The tw
stood motionless . . .

Their eyes were locked, and Rikki was struck by the energy they seemed to emit. Then Clay shrugged and turned to her. "Dinner tomorrow," he declared. "I'll call."

Beyond his shoulder she could see her father's face turning scarlet. Clay might not have taken over Strategix yet, but he acted as if he'd bought controlling interest in *her* stock!

"I don't think so," she said, her chin lifting a notch. She wouldn't be the rope in their stupid tug-of-war game.

But his hand came up to her jaw, cupped it to tilt her face higher. "Then think again," he told her.

He kissed her as if he had all the time in the world and no audience. Then he moved her aside, turning to nod to her father. "Evening, sir." And he left them, his strides long and jaunty as he returned to his waiting cab.

Peggy Nicholson, daughter of a Texas wildcatter, comes by her risk-taking naturally. Despite a fear of heights, she has dabbled in rock climbing and has been known to climb scaffolding to repaint her Rhode Island home when needed. She's been a teacher, an artist and a restorer of antique yachts. But her two main passions are sailing and writing, which, she insists, are all the better when combined. As Peggy says, "I can't imagine a nicer way to live."

Appropriately enough, final revisions for *Tender Offer* were done afloat in the Bahamas. "I wrote while the rest of the crew slept," Peggy confides, "starting well before dawn each morning."

Books by Peggy Nicholson

HARLEQUIN PRESENTS
732—THE DARLING JADE
741—RUN SO FAR
764—DOLPHINS FOR LUCK

HARLEQUIN SUPERROMANCE
193—SOFT LIES, SUMMER LIGHT
237—CHILD'S PLAY
290—THE LIGHT FANTASTIC

Don't miss any of our special offers. Write to us at the following address for information on our newest releases.

Harlequin Reader Service
901 Fuhrmann Blvd., P.O. Box 1397, Buffalo, NY 14240
Canadian address: P.O. Box 603,
Fort Erie, Ont. L2A 5X3

TENDER OFFER

Peggy Nicholson

Harlequin Books

TORONTO • NEW YORK • LONDON
AMSTERDAM • PARIS • SYDNEY • HAMBURG
STOCKHOLM • ATHENS • TOKYO • MILAN

ISBN 0-373-03009-6

Harlequin Romance first edition October 1989

TO JEFF

And with special thanks to
Bob, Marie, and Nicole Martin,
for their hospitality to a writer
in need of a desk
in a quiet corner.

CHAPTER ONE

"THAT'S IT! This is the limit. This is the last *straw*." Erika Casey made her announcement with an ominous precision that her students would have recognized. That tone of voice meant that you put your head down and got right to work. And did not even think of calling the popular young biology teacher "Red" for at least ten minutes. She rarely stayed angry longer than that.

"You said it, honey! Gridlocked at six-thirty. How's a guy s'posed to make a livin'..." The cab driver concluded that thought by mashing the taxi's horn again. Its indignant *bronnkkkk!* joined the chorus of frustration rising from all sides. Echoing off the brick and granite walls of the man-made canyons of midtown Manhattan, the racket seemed to double, then double again. The din grew to full orchestration, its horn section rising above the bass rumble of idling engines and the clash of truck gears. Over the distant rooftops, a yellow summer sky seemed to mock them all with a vision of unattainable freedom.

As her driver jabbed the horn again, Rikki bit her lip. Her outburst had not been inspired by the traffic jam—at least not directly. She'd been thinking of her father and the promise he had broken. She looked at her watch once more. It was 6:33 now. Her father had promised—had promised her—that he'd arrive home an hour ago. The party in celebration of his twenty-ninth wedding anniversary was due to start in precisely twenty-seven minutes. That might not mean beans to John Casey—after all, hadn't he always put business ahead of his marriage and family?—but to his wife, to Rikki's mother...

A vision of Elizabeth Casey's face, too white, too terrifyingly fragile since her heart attack last month, wavered before Rikki's eyes for an instant, blotting out the street of motionless vehicles. "This is it!" she declared. She dropped the twenty dollar bill she'd been holding on to the seat beside the driver. "It's faster to walk. Thanks, anyhow."

Weaving between the motionless cars, Rikki was too intent on the sidewalk ahead to note the yelp of approval from one young cab driver as she cut in front of his vehicle. Someone else wolf whistled. Rikki's eyes remained fixed on the river of pedestrians beyond the cars. John Casey always chose the east side of Fifth Avenue for his homeward walk. With his reddish brown hair, which she'd inherited, and his height, he was easy to pick out, even in such a crowd as this. But nowhere on this block could she see his uncompromisingly militaristic march, that familiar, impatient frown he wore when anything or anyone got in his way. And this was the last block before his office building. Since she'd scanned the sidewalks all the way from her parents' co-op in the East Seventies, that left only one place to find him—in his office.

"The last straw!" she promised as she whirled through the revolving door and into the lobby of his office building. Her high heels clicked out an exasperated tempo as she sailed across the marble lobby toward the elevators. The security man half rose from behind his desk, then subsided when he saw her face. "Evening, Miss Casey," he called respectfully.

She punched the elevator button, then spun to face him, the skirt of her dark green cocktail dress floating around her knees. "Hello, Henry. Have you seen my father?"

"Not today, Miss Casey—I just came on duty. But I see he logged in here at 7:30 this morning. Late for him."

She nodded rueful agreement, then turned as the elevator door opened. She had begged her father—pleaded—that he take some time off to be with her mother. "You nearly lost her!" she had reminded him only last week. "It's possible that you could lose her yet. Can't you take a short vacation, just stay home with her? It would mean so much to Mom."

But John Casey had had his excuses, as he had ever since Rikki had been old enough to form the question, "Where's Daddy?"

"This is a bad time," he'd told her stiffly. "There are rumors downtown that..." He'd stopped, then simply shrugged. "I can't cut out right now, Rikki. It's impossible." But he *had* shortened his normal eleven-hour working day by one hour, Rikki had noticed—an enormous concession for John Casey. So at least he had been making some sort of effort.

Until tonight, the night when it would have counted most of all.

Rikki glanced at her watch again, her ears popping slightly as the elevator rose. 6:45. Her mother's only guests, her best friend Anna and Anna's latest beau, would have arrived by now. The caterers hired for this special occasion were scheduled to start serving the hors d'oeuvres at 7:00. If the streets were still jammed once she'd coaxed him out of the building, could she possibly get him to take the subway? To the best of her knowledge, her father hadn't ridden the train in the last ten years. "He will tonight!" she vowed as the elevator stopped. She stepped out onto the top floor of the headquarters of the U.S. Strategix Corporation.

The desk facing the elevator door was empty. So the sleek receptionist, with her smile of cool inquiry, must have gone for the day. Apparently not all employees of Strategix shared its founder's legendary appetite for overtime.

Rikki wheeled in the direction of the executive suite, her long legs carrying her in a fluid stride that looked as if it should have been noiseless. But her heels clacked out a message of determination that would have telegraphed its warning to any but the most preoccupied of men.

Forming an ultimatum in her mind, Rikki did not hear the soft shuffle and creak of shoe leather at first. Then she looked up as a group of men turned the corner ahead and bore down on her.

Her eyes swept the five men hopefully, then dismissed them. Her father was not among them. It was just some group of businessmen, wearing their three-piece suits like the uniforms of some small and splendidly tailored army. She had an impression of polished shoes, leather brief cases, height, wide shoulders. They were grouped a bit more closely than seemed normal, like a military unit in hostile territory, presenting a phalanx of pinstripes on broad chests as they advanced.

But Rikki was far from impressed. At this hour of the day, they ought to be home. Somewhere out in the suburbs, women and children would be waiting for these men. Waiting with as much longing as she and her mother had waited for her father, all those years. For that matter, these men might be the reason her father had broken his promise this evening. Undoubtedly, they came straight from John Casey's office.

Her chin high, Rikki moved to the right to let them pass. "Rikki!"

She was moving too fast to respond right away. A hand shot out to close on her arm, half swinging her around. Her heel slipped on the polished floor, and the man's hand tightened, steadying her effortlessly as she wobbled. "Rikki."

Happy. Exasperation had turned to happiness so suddenly that she felt dizzy, staring up at this man's dazzling grin. Later, she would look back and marvel at how she had recognized him in so many ways, on so many levels before her brain put the bits together. But right now the sound of his voice saying her name, the warmth of his hand on her arm, even the subtle scent of his skin, simply told Rikki that she was happy in a way she hadn't been for years. The reason why lagged behind the emotion by several heartbeats, then her eyes snapped wide as it hit her. *Clay*—this was Clay McCann!

"Rikki," he repeated.

After all these years, just like that, here he was again! It was like turning around on a rainy day to find a rainbow arching overhead. Her lips parting eagerly, she swayed toward him, but the firm grip of his fingers on her arm checked that instinctive response.

As she stopped short, she could feel the blood sweeping into her face. Good heavens, what had she meant to do— walk right into his arms? The men who had stopped to cluster around them shifted uncomfortably, and eyed her with various expressions of interest or curiosity or approval.

"You don't remember me," Clay said as the silence lengthened. His grin faded.

That conclusion was so ridiculous that if she hadn't been speechless already, it would have rendered her so. She smiled and shook her head helplessly. Not remember him! He was engraved on her mind, from that expressive dip midway along his dark eyebrows to the shape of his bare feet, to the way there always seemed to be a hint of laughter shimmering behind his words. But now... This Clay didn't match her memory. He was bigger, brighter... not a child's lovesick daydream, but a large and very solid reality.

"Well—" the corners of his mouth took on a whimsical quirk "—I guess we'll just have to return to go and start over, then." His hand started to drop away, but she flung up her own to cover his fingers, keeping them pressed against her forearm.

"Clay, of course I remember you! It's just that I— That you— You've grown," she finished lamely. Had he ever! Clay McCann had been gorgeously gangly, all leg and raw-boned and big feet at twenty. But that had been eleven—no, twelve—years ago. He'd filled out beautifully—her eyes swept over his shoulders, his chest, then back up to his face.

He looked wonderful, but still she felt a moment of stinging loss. He was not the same, nor ever would be again. And just by standing there, he was routing all her memories, superimposing a new and larger reality on mental images that had grown soft and blurred over the intervening years. This Clay seemed not only larger, but somehow harder-edged than the boy she remembered.

Behind Clay a man shifted position. Another moved into the edge of her vision, and this one was smiling—they all were. As she took in the amusement of her audience, Rikki flushed scarlet again.

Clay seemed to notice his cohorts for the first time, as well. "You'll have to excuse us, Jim," he addressed one of the men. "This is turning into old home week, here. Wait for me in the lobby, will you?"

"But—" The man, who was almost as tall as Clay, started to object, then stopped himself. "Fine." Assuming command, he led the march toward the elevator.

"*I've* grown!" Clay resumed their conversation. "Look at you!" He did, in a swift all-over appraisal that warmed the blood singing through her veins. His hand tightened on her arm reflexively, then loosened again. "You were a stunner at fourteen, but now..." He shook his head in wordless admiration.

She laughed up at him. He had always known how to make her feel good, from the day they'd met. She remembered that first look of approval he'd thrown her as she had stepped aboard her father's corporate yacht, that summer day twelve years ago. His teeth had been as white as his first-mate's uniform, and he had snapped her a mocking salute that had made her smile as she was smiling now.

"What are you *doing* here?" she laughed. "The last I heard you were cutting a swath through Chicago!" *With a wife,* she remembered belatedly. The stab of dismay that followed this recollection wiped the smile from her face. Dear God, he was married! How could she have forgotten that? She'd gone around with a lump in her throat for a week after she'd heard.

Clay also had lost his grin and his eyes took on a steely cast. "I'm..." He glanced swiftly over his shoulder, toward the door to John Casey's office suite. When he turned back to her, his smile renewed itself. But now it had a reckless edge to it—an odd hint of hardness replaced the pure, uncomplicated joy of a moment ago. "I'm standing here asking you to come have a drink with me, Ms. Casey. And I want the story of your life as a grown-up lady while we're at it." Still holding her arm, he made a move toward the elevator.

Rikki stood still. There was nothing she wanted more in this world than to go with Clay, nothing at all, but—"I can't, Clay. Not tonight. I came here to see Dad." Once, that summer when the whole world revolved around Clay, she would have blurted out why. But he was right, she'd grown up. Grown up and grown away from him. You couldn't just pour out your troubles to someone who was virtually a stranger. And a married stranger at that.

"He's pretty busy right now, Rik. And I want to talk to you before—" Clay stopped and frowned. "He won't miss you just now," he said flatly. "Come have a drink, and I'll drop you off here in an hour or two."

Had she ever denied him anything in her life before? She was sure not. This was a first, and it felt all wrong. "I can't, Clay." She detached his hand and squeezed it, then dropped it hastily. "Rain check?"

His eyes narrowed for a second—he'd expected to win this dispute, apparently. Then he nodded. "My whole checkbook. But what about after you see him? A quick drink, just across the street if you haven't got time for anything nicer." His eyes scanned her party dress again, this time taking in its significance.

She hesitated, her longing written plain on her face. "I don't think I'll have time."

"Make the time." The tone was firm—an order given— but he touched the tip of her nose, the tiniest of caresses.

No one had done that to her for twelve years. She stifled an impulse to touch the spot where his finger had rested.

"I'll wait there for an hour," he continued. "O'Malley's, across the street." His eyes seemed to be adding some message of urgency to his words.

What was going on here? "I'll try," she agreed, troubled by that look.

"If I don't see you tonight, Rikki, I'll come looking for you," Clay warned. "I've been wondering how you were doing for a long, long time."

Could that really be true? She had always assumed that the wondering and remembering were on her part alone. "All right," she said softly, then simply stood there, robbed of all volition by his presence.

His eyebrows tilted in question, and she realized with a start that it was up to her to leave now. It took all her willpower to smile, then to turn and walk away from him.

Moving down the corridor, she felt as if she were wading through a knee-deep river, while the current did its best to sweep her back toward the man behind. Until she stepped through the door to her father's office, she could feel Clay's eyes upon her.

Rikki shut the office door, then leaned against it, suddenly glad to have a barrier between herself and his eyes. *Clay McCann* ... here, now, in her life again just like that, like a bolt from the blue. Reaction was starting to set in. She felt weak behind the knees, grateful for the door's support. *Clay McCann*... But how could he be affecting her like this? She'd gotten over him years ago... hadn't she?

Perhaps it wasn't him at all. She tried to remember when she'd eaten last. Skipping meals often made her shaky. But this was a different sort of light-headedness. A lightness of heart...

Rikki pulled a steadying breath, trying to fill that hollowness inside her with air. *Put him out of your mind,* she told herself sternly. *Remember Mom. Remember her party.* That's why she was here, after all. She blinked, then forced her eyes to focus on the room before her.

But if Rikki had been knocked off balance, then so had the rest of the world, apparently. She found herself surveying a scene of hushed pandemonium. Facing her across the room was Miss Zimmer's ferociously tidy desk. Her father's private secretary stood behind that desk, a telephone suspended in each hand near her ears while she held a hissing conversation with a young man whom Rikki didn't recognize. But with that conservative suit and tie, he was obviously a junior exec in her father's company. The man nodded vigorously in agreement with Miss Zimmer. He turned to leave the office, almost bumping into Rikki in the process. "E-excuse me!" he stammered as he slipped by her. She shut the door on the sound of his footsteps breaking into a run.

"Then you'll have to find him!" Miss Zimmer told one of the telephones. "Fly out there if you have to. The meeting starts at ten, but we'll want him sooner if possible." She hung up that phone, hit the button to switch to the second phone line, and the first phone rang again. Miss Zimmer let out a sniff—as close to a curse as Rikki had ever heard from her, rolled her eyes at Rikki and told the second phone line, "Would you hold again for a moment, please?" The answering squawk was ruthlessly punched into silence, then she picked up the ringing phone. "Mr. Casey's office—oh,

Mr. Bradley, thank you for calling in! I'm so sorry for the inconvenience . . ."

The door to John Casey's inner sanctum swung wide and Rikki's father filled the doorway. "Miss Zimmer, when in blue blazes are you going to get me Bradley?"

Miss Zimmer showed not an inkling of the triumph she must surely be feeling as she informed her boss that that member of the board of directors awaited his pleasure on line one at this very moment, while on line two . . .

"Dad?" Rikki ventured as he started to shut his door.

"Rikki!" John Casey saw her for the first time, though she had been standing only feet away. "Wait there." He pointed at a chair in the outer office.

"But—" His door closed, shutting her out. With a sigh Rikki sat. Her father had risen from buck private to captain's rank in the army before he quit to make his mark in the business world, and that had surely been the army's loss. He was born to command. No one resisted him when he used that tone. "What's going on?" she asked Miss Zimmer, but that lady was soothing the party on line two again.

Could Clay and his men have inspired this frenzy? Instinctively Rikki shied away from that question. Instead she glanced at her watch. 7:10. Her parents' twenty-ninth anniversary party had commenced by now. All it lacked was one-half the happy couple. Her eyes stung and she blinked them rapidly. *I don't care what's going on here. How can Dad do this to her?*

The door to the corridor opened, then an older man strode briskly into the room. He raised his bushy eyebrows in greeting to Miss Zimmer, gave Rikki a courteous smile, took in the closed door to her father's suite at a glance and settled on the couch on the opposite side of the room. A banker, Rikki decided, noting his impeccably understated attire. But he was keeping most uncharacteristic banker's hours.

But then this entire situation was uncharacteristic of Strategix. The business that John Casey had built from the ground up always ran on greased ball bearings, silently, efficiently, seemingly without effort—as long as one forgot to count the hours and years of effort that its founder poured into the whole operation. But drama and fuss were not her father's way. He hated fuss.

The phone connected to the inner office buzzed, and Miss Zimmer murmured into it. She hung up and smiled at the banker. "Mr. Feldstein? Mr. Casey will see you now."

But the older man had been trained in a school as stern as Rikki's father's, if one with a different set of values. He stood and walked across the room to Rikki. "Miss? You're John Casey's daughter, surely?" He held out his hand. "I've seen your pictures on your father's desk for years. I'm Sam Feldstein." He nodded toward the door as they shook hands. "You seem to be waiting, and I'm afraid my business may tie your father up for some time. Why don't you go ahead?"

Her father was not going to see it this way, she realized as she murmured her gratitude and headed for the inner office. Family always came second to business in a crisis. *But not this time!* she told herself. An image of her mother's face—the way she smiled when she was hiding a hurt—flashed across Rikki's mind for an instant. She shut the door behind her and went forward across the wide oriental rug, her chin defiantly high.

Her father was talking on the phone again. John Casey looked up to scowl at her, and in spite of herself, Rikki stopped in her tracks. Then he swivelled his chair to face the windows. Squaring her shoulders, she moved on past his desk to stand near the glass and gaze out.

The Empire State Building had taken on a ruddy glow where it rose above the shadows cast by the buildings that encircled it. It was almost sundown. The sun was setting on one more day in a life that might not have too many more.

One more day in which John Casey had found something more urgent to occupy his time than the woman he'd once sworn to love and cherish. *It won't be that way for me!* Rikki swore, not for the first nor the fiftieth time. She blinked fiercely and thought it again. *Not that way for me.*

The phone clicked down behind her. "What is it, Rikki? Can't you see I'm busy?"

She took a deep breath, but did not turn. It was harder to look him in the eye and defy him. "It's your wedding anniversary," she reminded him flatly.

He let out a prolonged and exasperated breath but didn't speak. Stubbornly she didn't turn to face him, and finally he sighed again heavily. "Rikki, I've got an emergency here."

Funny, how his emergencies were always business related. She stared out the window, a parade of broken promises gliding before her suddenly swimming eyes: her piano recital that he'd missed when she was eight. Her mother's birthday party that year when Rikki had grown old enough to recognize her mother's tears. The time she broke her wrist, and he couldn't come to the hospital. Her graduation from high school, then later from college. The Thanksgiving dinner she had cooked at her new apartment, only last year. These and a thousand other tiny, crucial, irreplaceable events when he'd been at the office or off on a business trip. But those occasions hadn't been emergencies in John Casey's book.

"Did you see young McCann?" he asked her out of the blue. "I don't know if you'd remember him. He crewed on the *Princess* the summer we sailed to Bermuda. And then he worked for me for a year or two, once he graduated from business school." John Casey let out a snort—as if at some memory, and he thumped his desk.

Rikki's smile was rueful. Without turning she nodded. So her father had never even noticed the wonderful, terrible, heart-wrenching crush she'd had for Clay that summer. That was so typical! Anyone, everyone else in the world, from the captain of the *Princess*, to her mother, to the waitress in that little café in Bermuda on that one wonderful day she and Clay had shared—everyone had been able to see the heart she'd worn on her sleeve for Clay McCann. Only her father... "Yes," she said finally. "I saw him. He wanted me to have a drink with him across the street..."

"Did he, by God!" John Casey's chair squealed as he shoved it back from his desk. Startled, Rikki glanced over her shoulder. He was on his feet already and moving fast. He reached her and swung her around. "Did you say yes?"

"No! Mom's waiting for us right now. Anna should be there by now, but imagine how you'd feel if you gave a party and nobody came?" She tried to draw her arm away. He was hurting her, and clearly he did not know it.

Her father ignored this gesture. "Rikki, I want you to go have that drink with McCann! Is it too late?"

What was going on here? Her father had never bothered to play matchmaker before. And now that she looked at him... Rikki stared. He had loosened his tie. She had never seen him do that before. Her father was a paragon of formality at the office. He always wore his suit jacket, and he *never* loosened his— Reaching up, she put the backs of her fingers to his cheek. "Are you all right, Dad?" There was a faint sheen of perspiration along his upper lip, but he felt cold to the touch, rather than feverish, and his eyes were overly bright.

He jerked his chin, shaking her hand aside. "I'm fine. Now, is it too late to see McCann?"

Something was very wrong here. "Why?"

Restlessly he turned away from her to prowl across to the window. Though he stared out, somehow she knew that he saw nothing. He wheeled to face her, his legs braced. "McCann's company has just threatened to buy us out, lock, stock and barrel," he announced bleakly.

Dear God—so that's what Clay had been up to!

"He offered to make me—me!—vice-president of the combined corporations. Under him, of course—the young...puppy! Why, I taught him everything he ever learned about business!"

Oh, God... "You're not going to accept..." she began, knowing the answer already.

John Casey's glare told her that this was no time for absurdities. "I told him to—" his voice trailed into silence. An officer and a gentleman did not swear in front of ladies. "His offer was totally inadequate and I told him so," he informed her coldly. Stalking past his daughter, he came up against the front of his desk, stood there staring sightlessly down at it, then swung to face her again.

"But then why would you want me to go drink with him?" Her question was carefully rational to match her father's tone of icy control. He would not want pity from her—now or ever—and she didn't offer it.

"Because this was only the first skirmish. McCann has been buying up our stock for weeks. We'd heard rumors that somebody was, but we couldn't find out who."

"So Clay's making a hostile tender offer?" Rikki was enough her father's daughter to know the language of corporate takeovers.

Her father's jaw muscles bunched as he nodded. "He makes the public announcement tomorrow. I don't think he really expected me to accept a friendly deal."

No, Clay was no fool. He knew that John Casey would sooner die than willingly sell his beloved corporation. If Clay wanted Strategix, he would have to take it. Her heart sank at the thought. So the battle would start tomorrow, when Clay officially announced his intentions to buy Strategix stock at some inflated price. If enough Strategix shareholders offered him their shares at that price, then Clay could buy control of her father's company. *But how could Clay do that to him?*

"You know what they call him on Wall Street these days?" her father asked.

Yes, she knew. Rikki had followed his career off and on, since he graduated from Harvard Business School. Whenever she was in the library, she looked up Clay's name in the guide to periodicals. His was the kind of personality that *Forbes* and *Fortune* magazine loved to cover—young, brash and stunningly successful.

"They call him Mac the Knife," her father continued bitterly. "Or Knife McCann. He's taken over four major companies in the last six years. Once he's bought them, he carves the divisions he doesn't want up into pieces and sells off their assets, piece by bleeding piece!" John Casey's gaze swept around his office, as if he expected to find one of Clay's price tags affixed to his massive desk. "Well, that's not going to happen to *my* company, by God! I'd sooner bomb Strategix back to the stone age than hand it over to Knife McCann." He swung back to his daughter. "So that's why I want you to go have a drink with him. This is war, and in a war, information is the ultimate weapon. We've got just fifteen days, starting tomorrow, before the Securities and Exchange Commission laws will let him purchase any more of our stock. I've got just fifteen days to beat McCann, and I'm going to need all the help I can get, Rikki."

No. For a long moment, Rikki stared in speechless dismay. *Oh, no, please!* Then she caught her breath. "Dad, Clay used to be a friend of mine. I can't—I can't spy on him. Besides," she added placatingly, "you and I have a party to go to."

It was doubtful he even heard that plea. For John Casey's face had gone rigid with her refusal. Her father never lost control of his temper, but Rikki found that she was holding her breath as she waited for the explosion that must surely come this time.

It did not. "So that's the way it is," he said after a thunderous silence.

"Yes..." It came out so weak that she swallowed, then tried it again. "Yes," she said more firmly. She would have to be a neutral in this war, couldn't he see that?

Then another thought hit her. Her father had made his millions. How many houses did one man need, after all? How many cars could he drive? How much food could he eat? If he never worked another day in his life, John Casey had earned enough to keep himself and his wife in luxury for the rest of their lives. Maybe he would learn to live, if he lost his company. Maybe he'd remember he had a wife who needed him, more now than ever.

Her father sighed and for a split second looked more hurt than angry. The sound caught at her heart, but as she put out a hand, he turned away from her and sat down heavily behind his desk. "Well, then..." He picked up a pencil and put it down again. "If that's the way it is..." He touched the pencil, rolling it an inch or two along the desktop. "Give your mother and Anna my apologies. And make sure she doesn't try to wait up for me. I've got an emergency meeting at ten." He picked up his phone.

Rikki moved before she thought, pressing her finger down on the disconnect button of the phone and holding it down. "Dad, you promised you'd be there tonight. Don't do this to Mom!"

His brows came together sharply, and Rikki snatched her hand away as if it had been burned. Casey hung up the phone with an ominous gentleness. "Rikki, all bets, all promises, are off in a war."

"And if the first casualty is your wife?" She spread her hands flat on his desk and leaned toward him, willing him to see it her way, her green eyes fiercely pleading. *Please. Don't do this!*

Her father swallowed, started to speak, then stopped.

Rikki waited. *If you love her, then don't...*

"Would you consider a trade?" he asked abruptly. "I need a clean shirt. This meeting will last all night, once we get the board of directors rounded up. What if I...go home for that shirt, and stay with your mother until—" he glanced at his watch "—nine forty-five. If I did that, would you go talk to McCann for me?"

It was so unfair! He'd thrown the responsibility for her mother's happiness back in Rikki's lap. She felt a twinge of admiration along with her dismay—he was a negotiator, all right! "I *can't*, Dad. He's a friend. I can't spy."

"No one's asking you to spy, Rikki. Just remember any information that McCann is willing to give out. He may talk freely to you, might even brag, if he drinks a bit. I need to know if his company has the cash on hand to buy us out, or if they're borrowing. Is he serious about this takeover, or is this just a bluff? With his reputation, it could be that he's just hoping we'll roll over and wave our legs when he comes calling. If we don't, then he might not fight, he might just go on to his next victim. Just listen to him, Rikki, that's all I'm asking."

"That's all?" It was all in the world she wanted to do, listen to Clay McCann.

"That's all." As he looked up at her, her father's face was hard and unmoving as a rock. Only his eyes pleaded his case.

Turning away from that unflinching demand, Rikki pressed two fingertips between her eyebrows, where it was starting to ache. What harm could she really do, listening to Clay? He was far too intelligent to give out harmful information to the daughter of his takeover target. And *he* wouldn't put her in a position like that, even if her own father would. She turned back again. "And if I do, you'll go straight home to Mom?"

"I promise," her father said, his face settling into lines of satisfaction.

For whatever promises are worth in war time! Rikki thought, calculating swiftly. Her mother would miss her at the party, but two hours of her husband's rare and precious time would more than make up for her daughter's absence, especially on this occasion....

"Well?"

It was a complex equation, requiring that she balance her mother's pleasure, her father's need, her own moral queasiness against a doubtless unwise but nevertheless unshakable desire on her part simply to see Clay one more time. *All right.* She found that she was nodding, the decision reached on some level deeper than words before she voiced it. "All right, Dad. You've got a deal. Want to walk out with me now?"

Her father looked startled, as if the consequences of his side of the bargain were just hitting home. "I can't. I'll have to talk with Sam Feldstein for a minute or two first. You go on ahead without me."

Rikki nodded. That was easy enough. After all, wasn't that what she'd been doing ever since she could walk alone?

CHAPTER TWO

THE FEELING returned in the elevator, on her way down. That sickening, wonderful feeling Rikki hadn't felt since the summer so long ago. She'd always gotten it on her way to look for Clay...an eagerness—no, a need—to reach his side that seemed to intensify with every step that she took toward her goal. Hunger combined with fear, that was what it had felt like—and felt like now. As if something that you wanted—that you needed desperately—was just beyond your fingertips and receding into the distance even as you ran after it, arms outstretched.

The elevator bumped to a gentle halt, and Rikki stood still for an instant, staring bleakly into space. *I can't feel like that again! That was just a teenage crush. I got over it years ago. I don't want to feel that way again.*

The feeling twisted in her stomach and she hurried out of the elevator. Clay would be gone. He would not have waited. He would have walked off into the clamor and endless confusion of the city. And she would be left to chase down street after crowded street, searching for those wide shoulders and that head of thick tawny hair, those long, careless strides that would always keep him three steps ahead of her, no matter how fast she ran.

She was nearly running as she left the building.

He'll be gone, Rikki told herself again, as she opened the door to O'Malley's. She paused in the doorway. It was a men's bar if ever she'd seen one—dark, smoky and suddenly raucous as a tiny figure on the TV screen over the bar hit a long bouncer to center field.

A tall figure loomed up out of the shadows. "Rikki, I was about to give up."

Maybe you should have, she thought as he caught her elbow and steered her out the door. Maybe it would have been best for them both if she hadn't come. It had taken her years of pain and longing to get over her childhood crush for this man. To risk falling under his spell again, now that he was married, was sheer idiocy. All the same, the feeling was completing itself as it always had on those wondrous occasions when she'd gone searching for Clay and had actually found him. The hunger, the fear were turning to a warm, glowing relief, as if he'd opened his arms and hugged her close. As if she were home—home and safe at long last. Her spirits rocketed skyward, and suddenly Rikki wanted to laugh with sheer relief. Just for the joy of it.

"Not your kind of place," Clay explained, nodding at the bar as he led her out to the sidewalk.

"How do you know what's my kind of place, Clay?" He was right, that bar wasn't, but how did he know? How much did he really remember about her? Memory depended so much on the significance of the event to the rememberer. And she had no doubt that summer had meant much more to her than it ever had to Clay.

"Has your taste changed all that much?" He considered her for a moment, as if her answer to the question would be an important one. "If I took you back to that little hole-in-the-wall café in St. George, would you know it was a hole in the wall this time?"

Try me she almost said. Instead she shook her head, smiling. So he remembered that, at least. That had been the happiest day of her life, bar none.

Clay glanced over her shoulder, then raised his hand with authority. "Taxi!" Rikki turned to see the rare sight of an unoccupied cab pulling in to the curb for them.

Their taxi driver was a talkative one. He'd come recently from Haiti, and he wanted to know what lay north of New York City. Clay could have easily snubbed the man; instead he responded at length with useful information.

Rikki leaned back to watch. Clay was as patient with this man as he'd been with her that summer so long ago. She must have seemed such a pest, the way she'd tagged him everywhere around the boat.

But he'd never made her feel that way. He'd accepted her worship with humor and tact. His big brother friendliness had been the perfect response. He'd taught her to tie bowlines and half hitches, how to read the radar in the wheelhouse. She'd come to him for love that he could not give, but he'd given her friendship and shown her how to tell weather by the clouds and the wind. He'd let her bring him coffee when it was his turn at the helm—why he'd probably nearly drowned with all the coffee she'd brought him—but he'd never once complained. He'd let her sit with him in the red glow of the night-lit wheelhouse and had let her talk to him hour after hushed hour while the *Princess* shouldered her way through the long offshore swells.

He'd cared for her that summer. Clay had never loved her, but he'd cared. That had almost been enough.

And that's why she was back here, she realized, turning to study his hawk-nosed profile. Because she still needed a friend. Because he still was her friend, even after all the years. She knew it the moment he spoke.

"Yes, you would like it in Rhode Island," Clay was assuring the worried driver for the third time. "It would be a good place to raise a family. Not as big, not as dangerous as New York."

"Yes!" The driver nodded rapidly. "Yes, that is just what I want, such a place! I thank you. I will go see it." He pulled the car to the curb and Rikki dragged her eyes off Clay to find where he'd taken her. The massive base of the World

Trade Towers filled the windows of the cab and rose out of sight.

"This is a long way from Bermuda," she observed as they crossed the wide plaza that surrounded the buildings.

"Yes." The sleeve of Clay's dark blue business suit brushed her bare arm. Its touch sent a shiver spiraling up her spine. "We've both come a long way since then."

And he didn't just mean miles, she realized, or even years. He'd changed. She could sense it, but not define it as yet. A kind of hardness, was that it? Or was it just his size that gave her that impression? No, it had to be more than his size, for some large men were soft as overgrown teddy bears. But not this one. His arm brushed her again and she shivered inwardly.

"And you're a long way from home, aren't you?" he continued easily. "I heard you'd moved to Rhode Island years ago. That you were teaching science in a high school up there."

"You heard right," she agreed, wondering how he'd heard it at all. "But I've been here for a visit for over a month now."

"Must be nice to have your summers off." A note, not of envy but perhaps wryness, had crept into his voice.

Rikki did not notice. She was wondering if she should tell him about the reason for her extended visit, her mother's heart attack. Would that make any difference to his takeover plans? And did she really want to change those plans?

When she was a child, she had fantasized about her father quitting his job, or at least, finding a normal nine to five job like most fathers seemed to have. Once she'd grown up, moved away and made a life of her own, that old wish had lost much of its urgency. But now here it was again, as bright and shining as if she'd dreamed it only yesterday.

And now it seemed the ideal solution to the problem of her mother. Because Rikki would not be able to keep her company for too much longer. She couldn't put her own life on "hold" forever. At the very most, she could stay until summer vacation ended, but after that she had a job and a life of her own to get on with. So, if just when Elizabeth Casey needed support and companionship most, her husband might finally be freed to give it to her—

Coming back to the present with a start, Rikki found Clay's eyes upon her. Quickly she looked away, then up, as they continued walking. "I haven't been here in years." The city's tallest buildings loomed overhead, twin pillars seeming to hold up a sky filled with fire-streaked, streaming clouds. Then, with awful, majestic slowness, the towers began to topple over upon her. "Oh!"

Clay caught her as she swayed. "Easy there!" His arm slid around her waist and he pulled her to a stop, swinging her around to face him.

Laughing, embarrassed, she wobbled on her heels, then leaned against him, one hand spread wide against the solid warmth of his chest.

And for just a heartbeat, everything seemed to stop— time, the clouds overhead, her breathing...even his? No, one thing moved—his heart beneath her palm, with a rhythm that seemed to surge even as she noted it. Catching her balance, she pushed herself upright. "Sorry!" Her hand tingled. Closing it into a fist at her side, she felt she'd captured something too precious for words. "I'm sorry. I never can resist doing that, and I always get dizzy when I do. This time I really thought they were going to fall!"

Clay had not released her. "Still up there," he assured her, his eyes never leaving her face.

She had been babbling, hadn't she? She turned out of his arms and started walking.

He caught up in a stride or two. "You were afraid of heights," he said after a moment. "I'd forgotten that."

"And believe me, I've tried to," she assured him with a laugh, relieved to be back on safe ground again. Clay had put her up the *Princess*'s main mast in a bosun's chair to do some small chore for him. She'd been too proud to tell him how heights scared her.

"You were greener than a frog before I realized what was going on and got you down." He laughed quietly.

From the direction in which he was steering her, Rikki deduced where they were going—the Windows on the World, one of the most expensive and fashionable restaurants in the city. Surely Clay didn't feel the need to impress her? Or had he simply become used to places like this?

That summer on the *Princess*, he hadn't had two nickels to rub together. He'd been saving for his sophomore year in college. His family had been helping pay for the tuition, as she remembered, but Clay's contributions to the cost had been vital.

"You know—" She stopped and he stopped beside her. "Do you know what I'd like more than going up to the Windows, Clay? If we go up there, we'll have to just sit, and the music will make it hard to talk." And though she hated to admit it, she was afraid to try to carry on a conversation with Clay across a table. It would seem too formal, too like a date. They had always done things, when they had been together before. It was easier to talk to someone if his eyes were on the course of his boat, or the line he was splicing. "Besides, I've been there before." With her father, once, and some of his business associates. They'd talked finances until she could have wept with boredom.

"So where then?" Clay didn't look annoyed at all. Simply amused by her earnestness.

"Well, I've never gotten the nerve to go up to the outside Promenade Deck. Maybe with you here... I've always wondered about the wind...it's got to be awfully strong up there, hasn't it?"

His eyes crinkled slowly. "And I'm supposed to keep you from blowing off the top of the tower?" He threw back his head and laughed, then put a hand to the small of her back. "You always were the craziest kid, Rikki. This way."

Rikki had been as high as the glassed-in observation deck before. It was the open roof above that she'd never had the nerve to visit. But like many acrophobics, she was fascinated by the very thing that she feared. On the final escalator to the rooftop she edged closer to Clay.

As they stepped outside, he dropped a casual arm around her shoulders. "Think you can stand it?"

"Oh!" It wasn't what she'd imagined at all. The view was stunning, outrageous but— "I thought we'd be able to walk—or rather crawl—right out to the edge and look down over the side!" They stood on a catwalk built above the roof and set in a good twenty feet from the edges of the building. She could look out for miles in any direction, but the view straight down was hidden. To get close to the edge, she would have had to jump onto the roof, then scale a chain-link fence topped with barbed wire.

"Nope." Though she was in no danger of falling or even being blown—the breeze was surprisingly gentle and mild up here—Clay kept his arm around her. He pulled her gently into motion. "They knew better than to build it like that. They weren't about to let people like you, who can't even look up at a building, try to look down from this one."

"And no wind!" she marveled.

"No wind tonight," he agreed, smiling down at her. "You're safe."

She felt safe, and so totally in danger at the same time, that all she could do was nod. The air was cooler than she'd thought at first, and Clay's arm was wonderfully warm. She would be safe as long as he held her. The danger came from her wish that he'd hold her forever.

They strolled over to the waist-high railing and stood, staring out at the vast harbor. The Statue of Liberty was a slim, copper-green shape in the twilight, her lamp sharp and bright as the first star. Beyond her glittered the long curving pendant of the Verrazano bridge, all delicate filagree and aquamarine lights. To the west, the sun was sinking in a lurid swirl of smog and purple cloudbank over New Jersey. It branded itself on her eyes when she looked—she closed them and found its red-orange image pulsing inside her.

"You haven't grown so much," Clay said at her ear. "It was the heels that fooled me. Grown out a bit but not up more than an inch, I'd say."

"Thanks, I think!" She turned, laughing, to find his face heart-stoppingly close, encircled by the last fiery afterimage of the sun. She would have stepped back if his arm hadn't held her there.

"In all the right places," he assured her. "You were a skinny little thing." He shook his head slowly. "I can't quite believe you're here."

"Why shouldn't I be?" But she could name half a dozen reasons, starting with his wife and ending with her own peace of mind.

"Because you talked to your father first."

"Oh... Yes." So there it was, out in the open at last. Rikki met his eyes squarely. "Do you really mean to tender for Dad's company tomorrow?"

Clay's gaze was unflinching. "I do."

She took a deep breath, conscious of the way she moved against his arm as she did so. "He'll fight you, you know, down to his last paperclip."

The warning didn't seem to worry Clay. "I know." His arm tightened around her. "But what I don't know is...how *you* feel about all of this?"

Torn... It might be the best thing that ever happened to her father, but why, oh why, did it have to be Clay that would do it to him? If it could be done at all—Rikki found it almost impossible to conceive of her father without his company.

"Well?" Clay prodded.

"You're my friend, Clay..." She hesitated, choosing her words. "You always have been." But then, hadn't he been her father's friend as well? At least, he'd worked for him for a year after business school. "I don't know," she said un-happily. "You know how I've always hated the business."

"Yes, I know." She'd told him all about it that summer, how much it hurt, having an absentee father. How rejected both she and her mother felt, meaning less to him than his work. Clay had seen the situation for himself. Their cruise to Bermuda had proved to be a disaster, at least for Rikki's mother. For it had been Elizabeth Casey's idea to use the yacht, newly acquired in some business merger, to lure her husband into taking a vacation.

But John Casey had turned the *Princess* into a floating office. The two poor senior executives that he'd invited along had probably worked longer hours on that so-called vacation than they'd been accustomed to working at head-quarters in New York City. At least in the city, they'd had the option of escaping their boss at the end of the work day. One of them had even been seasick for most of the voyage, and paperwork is brutal on a queasy stomach.

If the wives had been less than thrilled by this ruthless monopolization of their husbands' vacation time, Eliza-beth Casey had been utterly mortified on their behalf. And furious with her husband. There had been fights—or at least as close as Rikki's parents ever came to fighting—all the way out to Bermuda and all the way home again.

That was how Rikki had come to have that wonderful day ashore with Clay. He'd plucked her off the boat, from the midst of the bitterest dispute her parents had ever had, as far as she remembered. He'd simply taken her hand and marched. He'd rented a motor scooter for two, and they had explored Bermuda from one lovely end to the other. Rikki had decided Clay was a magician that day, to turn misery to joy as he had. She would follow a man who could do that anywhere.

He had been looking at her for quite some time, Rikki realized all at once. She swung away to stare out over the harbor and the silver-blue roadstead beyond. Several ships

rode at anchor out there, all of them weather-cocked to face
the gentle sea breeze. A breeze seemed to feather across her
skin, stroking each nerve ending to a quivering awareness of
the man beside her. "So, where's your wife?" she asked with
brittle gaiety.

Clay started, and she felt him glance down at her, but she
didn't turn. "My ex-wife, you mean? Damned if I know,
Rikki. Or care. She was out in California, the last I heard,
hoping to break into the movies."

His words took a moment to sink in. When they did, she
wanted to laugh—could feel the laughter of sheer relief
bubbling up inside her. But that wasn't right, when Clay
might be hurting. "I see." She risked a quick look at him
and found that he wore the slightest twist of a smile. The
expression might have been amusement, might have been a
brave face put on the matter. She studied the ships again.
"Does it hurt?"

"Not anymore. It's been three years now, Rik. Now it
only hurts in the wallet. She took a nice consolation prize
with her when she left."

"She was—is—very beautiful. I happened to— I saw a
photo of you two together in a magazine once—just turned
the page and there you were." *You're protesting too much,*
she warned herself.

"Yes, Diana is gorgeous," Clay said shortly.

Gorgeous ... Yes, she was all of that. And just how important was beauty in a woman to him? Rikki didn't know.
That was one topic she'd been too shy to quiz him about that
summer. She'd wondered passionately, miserably, if he had
a girl somewhere. Worshiping him as she had, she'd been
jealously certain that every other girl in the world who saw
him would covet him as she did. Sometimes when she'd gone
to the 79th Street Boat Basin, where the *Princess* was
berthed, Clay had been off duty and gone. Had there been
some gorgeous girl in the city with whom Clay had passed
his free time? And how could that suspicion still hurt her so

now? It was not as if she'd had any claim on him. None but friendship.

As if the recollection of his divorce made him restless, Clay straightened and pulled her away from the railing. They strolled around to the east side of the catwalk to inspect Brooklyn. In this direction all the lights were on as night rolled up the sky. Draped across the gray, wrinkled throat of the East River, the Brooklyn Bridge was a dowager's necklace, dripping with diamonds. A tug boat steamed downriver, towing a string of black barges to the sea.

"And how about you?" Clay asked. "I tried to call you, two, no, it was three years ago..."

"You did?" Startled, she looked up at him, but his eyes were on the river.

"Called about ten, a Saturday morning. I'd heard from a friend of your mother's—Anna Wiley—that you were up in Rhode Island, teaching school. A guy answered. He was pretty surly. Said you were down in the basement, doing laundry, and to try back later."

She took a deep breath. "And you didn't."

"No, I didn't."

His unspoken question hung between them while she searched for words. Some strange, wild sort of hope was nattering at the back of her mind, and she beat it off frantically. This didn't mean— Just because Clay wondered who Peter was didn't mean that he was interested in her in any way outside of friendship. To entertain such a ridiculous hope and then to have it dashed down would be more than she could bear. "That must have been Peter," she said finally.

Peter had often stopped in for coffee on Saturday mornings. They had been next door neighbors, after all, and friends. For a while she'd even thought that they'd become much more than friends. She had warmed to him, Rikki realized now, because Peter had seemed to be everything that her father was not—reckless, unambitious, playful. He'd been a young chef, talented, but easygoing, with time enough to share life and love with her.

But somehow it had not worked out that way. Looking back on the relationship she saw now that it had been a little...flat. There had been something essential missing.

What she had first seen as Peter's charming spontaneity had looked, on closer scrutiny, to be something more like aimlessness. She'd considered him easygoing at first. Later she'd wondered if a better term for the trait might be slothful. In short, she'd found that she wanted drive in her man. She just didn't want that drive to be forever driving him away from her.

Why can't I find a man who knows what he wants? And who wants something reasonable? Not a business empire but something I could share in? Well, anyway, that man had not been Peter.

"Peter is history," she said lightly. Though it hadn't been that easy, letting go of him. She spun away from the railing and walked on, heading for the uptown side of the building.

Clay joined her after a moment. "Sorry. I didn't mean to pry."

Staring at the jeweled spires of midtown she shook her head. "That's okay, Clay. There's nothing there to pry into." She nodded at the Empire State Building. "Do you ever wonder if she gets jealous, not being number one anymore?"

He laughed and put a hand lightly on her arm. "No, I never did."

If she looked to the left of the Empire State Building, her father's office should be about...there. There were too many lights on to be sure which floor was Strategix headquarters, but that was roughly the place. How many people would be there now, scrambling to find some way to stop this man beside her? She shivered and suddenly had a dizzying, disorienting sense that she stood on the rim of a vast

chasm. Below her yawned the echoing depths of shadowed
stone and the tiny, crawling lights of the cars. Her eyes fastened on a rectangle of light, high up on the edge of a
building—there, there it was. There was the other rim of the
chasm, the other camp. But what was she doing over here,
on this side? This time her shiver racked her whole body.

"You're cold." Clay shrugged out of his coat. "Here."
He ignored the shake of her head and draped the garment
around her shoulders.

"I'll smother!" she protested, as he caught the lapels of
the coat and pulled it snugly around her. Reminding her of
the ocean, the warm smell of his skin enveloped her suddenly. He was still using the same after-shave he'd used at
twenty. She inhaled luxuriously, feeling comfort and joy
tingle out along her veins all the way to her fingertips,
sweeping all worries before it. How odd, how strange, to be
able to pick up with him where they had left off. How wonderful... *That's what I'm doing here.*

"What?" Clay asked, smiling down at her. He tugged
gently on the coat lapels, swaying her toward him.

It was impossible to voice what she was feeling. She shook
her head and rocked back on her heels. He held her there
suspended for a moment, his eyes holding her as much as his
hands, then he let her go. "Let's look at New Jersey," she
suggested and moved on. But what she really looked at,
once his eyes were on the last shreds of the sunset, was Clay.
The shape of his body showed clearly through the beautifully tailored shirt that he wore. He had definitely filled out.
Must be doing some sort of weight training—not to excess,
but enough to stay hard and trim. She had not been blind
with infatuation at fourteen. He was still a beautiful man.

After they'd admired the lilac haze and golden glitter of
New Jersey, they retreated to the glassed-in deck below.
Rikki was starving, and Clay bought them each a hot dog
and a beer at the snack bar on that level.

"Serves you right for passing up the Windows of the World," he told her with an unsympathetic grin.

As if the food mattered, when she was with him. "We wouldn't have had time to do it justice, anyway. And I ought to be home by ten at the latest." Her father would have gone back to his office by then. "There's the Foo—I'll have to walk her when I get home."

"Foo?" Clay reached up with a napkin to wipe a dab of mustard off her cheek.

It's no use, Rikki, she told herself as she wrinkled her nose and submitted to this big brotherly gesture. *When he looks at you, he still sees a fourteen-year-old kid.* But that wasn't the way Clay's touch made her feel! "Foo is Mom's miniature poodle—Felicity to Mom. Dad took to calling her the Foo-foo, and I'm afraid it stuck."

"I see . . . well, if I'm going to get you home on time, I guess we'd better be moving." Clay stood up from the bench they'd chosen overlooking the harbor, then pulled her to her feet. "I suppose it's for the best anyway. I have to meet some people at ten."

Ten—the same time her father would be holding his emergency meeting of the board of directors. Rikki studied him from the corner of her eye as they headed for the elevator. "A late party?" she hazarded and held her breath.

"Hardly!" he laughed. "A couple of lawyers, my investment banker and his assistants, my senior execs . . ." He glanced at her sharply and went silent.

His takeover crew. Just as her father would be plotting defensive moves tonight, Clay would be plotting the moves to swallow U.S. Strategix whole. The elevator started its drop, and for an instant she felt as if she'd left her stomach behind, floating in midair, while the rest of her plunged down the shaft. What had she been thinking of, tonight? Or rather not thinking of, as hard as she could avoid the thoughts? Clay meant to take Strategix—*take* it!

She'd been seeing Clay through memory's eyes, that's what she'd been doing. Seeing him as her beloved twenty-year-old first mate, not as he was now. Rikki looked up to find that he was watching her with an odd wariness in his eyes—a guarded look that was totally alien to the boy she had once known. She shivered again, suddenly chilled. How could that boy have grown up to be a taker?

"What is it?" Clay asked, as they stepped out of the elevator.

He was so quick to pick up on her moods—that had not changed at least. "Nothing," she said brightly.

Those dark, level eyebrows over his deep-set blue sailor's eyes drew together, but he didn't persist.

"Did you ever sail much, after your summer on the *Princess*?" she asked to distract them both, as they walked out onto the plaza.

That set him off on a series of sea stories that lasted them through the taxi ride to her parents' co-op in the East Seventies. As Clay talked, Rikki found her spirits rising again in spite of her misgivings. She didn't try to analyze why, simply gave herself up to the pleasure of his voice and his closeness. She would worry later, not now. Now was all too precious and fleeting.

When the cab pulled up in front of the door, Clay got out with her. "Wait here," he instructed their driver.

She had expected him to say good-night there on the sidewalk. But when he did not, when Clay accompanied her past the doorman and into the lobby, Rikki found her anxiety returning with a vengeance. It was 9:50. What if her father had not left yet? He might have pushed her into this meeting with Clay, but all the same, he would not be expecting her to bring the enemy home to his own doorstep! She cringed at the very idea of witnessing an encounter between the two men she— Rikki choked off that thought. It was a dangerous line of thought, promising pain. Startled by it, she looked up to find Clay studying her face.

He saw too much—would see things she'd never dream of telling him, if he looked too closely. Rikki turned her back on him to jab the elevator button.

"Rikki." Clay touched her shoulder.

She flashed a nervous smile over her shoulder at him but didn't turn back. "I'm late. Foo will be eating the drapes by now."

The elevator door opened. Clay caught the edge of the door and held it back for her. She stepped inside, turned to say good-night and found him entering the car. Oh, murder, he couldn't walk her to her door! If her father stepped out to find himself face to face with Clay—

"Which floor?" Clay asked. She wet her lips, then told him, and he pressed the button. "I'll help you walk the Foo," he said quietly. "You shouldn't do that by yourself, this time of night."

She shook her head. "It's all right, Clay. Harry, the doorman, keeps an eye on us. We just walk as far as the nearest tree, when it's this late. And you'll be late for your meeting." A meeting that started at ten. Why, he kept business hours as brutal as her dad's! The door slid open, and Rikki stepped toward it.

"Rikki." Clay caught her arm.

Oh, God, this was new territory. In all their time together, she'd never heard this husky note in his voice. A warm, tingling awareness rippled out from where his fingers held her. Her whole body was acknowledging his, all her nerves standing to attention and begging for more— more than just his hand on her arm. She stared up at him helplessly, and the elevator door closed.

Without letting her go, Clay touched a button and the car started to rise. He drew her to him, gently, irresistibly. "I'll say good-night here, I think." Warm and steady, his hand laced into her hair and he tilted her head back.

"Good night, then," she murmured, hoping to forestall what was coming. She wanted his kiss so, and dreaded it. It would change everything. Perhaps ruin every memory she held dear. "It's been nice . . ."

Just above her, his face crinkled into a slow grin. He was laughing at her—silently. "Yes," he agreed, his voice rough. He kissed the corner of her mouth.

His touch was experimental . . . considering . . . as if he savored a new wine—his touch pierced right through her. She inhaled sharply.

Her heart was slamming against her ribs now. Her hands spread tentatively, luxuriously, against the heat of his chest, then clenched spasmodically on his lapels. As she rose on her tiptoes, their kiss deepened, was suddenly not so gentle, and the elevator door slid wide.

"Oh, my!" The exclamation was elderly and female. Rikki tore her mouth free, turned her head to find a tiny, blue-haired matron goggling back at her from the hallway of the top floor.

"My sentiments exactly," Clay assured the woman. "Please excuse us." He hit the elevator button and the door closed. The car started down. Laughing, Clay pulled her close again. "My, oh, my, little Ms. Casey. How you have grown up."

"Idiot!" she told him, laughing herself, as he brushed his lips back and forth across her cheek. She twisted in his arms to hit the button for her floor, just before they would have passed it by.

"Crazy," Clay agreed. "Have supper with me tomorrow?"

The car stopped, and she reached back to press and hold the Door Open button. If she were to see him again—should she see him again? When he was attacking her father? She needed time to think.

"Supper tomorrow," he repeated when she didn't go on.

And it wasn't only that. It was one thing to love him from afar, to have him as a cherished friend. But this was new territory he was asking her to explore with him. And she could sense the danger even though she could not bring her thoughts to bear on it at this glorious moment. "I don't think I—"

"Then don't think. Say yes," he demanded. Clay's smile was still in place, but that wary look she'd noticed earlier was starting to kindle in his eyes. He looked no longer playful, but...formidable. A large, overwhelmingly male stranger, very used to getting what he wanted.

The elevator bell chimed—someone was summoning the car, probably the woman they'd shocked on the top floor. "I've got to go," she said quickly as she backed out of his arms. "And you're late for your meeting."

Clay shrugged, his eyes still assessing her. "There's no hurry. It will last all night."

Yes, no doubt it would... Was it that realization that was whispering *Danger* in the back of her brain, even while she longed to step back into his arms and kiss him again?

"I don't know, Clay. I—" The bell chimed again, then again as someone pressed and held the button. Rikki stepped into the corridor.

"I'll call you tomorrow," Clay said.

"Maybe you—"

"Tomorrow." He blew her a kiss and the door closed between them. She stood there for a moment, staring at the blank metal surface that had taken his place.

Her hand rose to her lips, and she fingered them absently, delicately, as if they were not her own, but another's. Slowly her lips formed a smile. In spite of all her worries, happiness was spinning like a top inside her. She had finally, after all these years of wishing and fantasizing, been kissed by Clay McCann.

It had been worth the wait.

CHAPTER THREE

RIKKI'S STATE of enchantment lingered on after her home-coming.

Her mother had gone to bed, and her father had re-turned to his office. Only Anna Wiley, her mother's friend, and a frantic poodle were there to greet her when she drifted into the apartment. And if Anna noticed Rikki's flushed cheeks, or the silly, dazed smile that kept breaking into view no matter how Rikki tried to concentrate on the conversa-tion at hand, she diplomatically kept her thoughts to her-self. The Foo had more urgent concerns.

After Rikki had walked the tiny dog and said good-night to Anna, she wandered out the French doors onto the ter-race. Her arms braced, she leaned out over the stone bal-ustrade, her eyes on the darkened street five stories below, her mind six hundred miles away. Overhead, a warm, lan-guid breeze stirred the leaves of the Japanese maple in its big stone planter. The sound transformed itself into the sigh of a Bermudian trade wind sifting through the needles of a casuarina tree—she and Clay had lain under such a tree for part of that day, while they dried off after a swim. They had lain not side by side as lovers lie, she remembered, but as children who are best friends lie, at angles to each other, their heads nearly touching, their eyes on the swaying branches above. Their words, when they bothered to speak, had been dreamy and slow. Clay had told her his secret plan under that tree, something he'd never told anyone else, he said. He meant to own his own boat someday, a yacht even

swifter and lovelier than the *Princess*. And he would sail her
right around the world. Then maybe, once he came back to
his starting point, if he felt like it, he might just sail around
a second time.

"If you ever need crew..." she had volunteered reck-
lessly. Clay had laughed, reached over his head to pat her
cheek and assured her that if he ever needed a first mate, she
was the first person he'd hire. She'd treasured his joking
assurance for years...

Inside, the phone rang. Rikki spun away from the balustrade, anxious that it not wake her mother. What if, by some
miracle, it was Clay? Her heart pattered as fast as her feet
while she ran to answer it.

But the voice that greeted her, when she picked up the receiver, was her father's. "Rikki, what did you learn?" His
voice was that of the military commander, demanding a re-
port from one of the troops.

Half her mind was still in Bermuda, and it would rather
have stayed there than deal with this. "Nothing, Dad," she
said at last.

"Nothing?"

"Well..." There was no way to soften the news. "Nothing, except that I don't think he's bluffing. I think Clay will
tender for you tomorrow."

There was a long pause, then her father sighed. That tiny,
almost inaudible exhalation conveyed all the worry that his
face would never have revealed to her. Hearing that sigh,
Rikki felt a sharp and sudden chill. Her mother would be
happier if he retired, but what would retirement do to her
father? "Dad—" She put forth a hand, as if she could touch
him, sooth him—something she would not dare to do, if he
stood before her.

"Where was he going when he left you, did he say that?"
John Casey's voice was back in control, its edges even
harder for the slip that had come before.

Her hand dropped slowly to her side. If she answered that question, was she betraying Clay? She felt like a woman on a tightrope. "He . . . he had some meeting to go to."

"With who?" her father barked.

"He didn't name names." Reluctantly, she repeated the titles of the men Clay had mentioned. That could not hurt Clay in any way that she could see.

Apparently her father agreed. There was a dissatisfied grunt from his end of the line. "Did he . . . say anything about seeing you again?"

For a moment she was choked with outrage. That he could think of using her, of exploiting her affection for Clay in this way— But then, to even think of doing so, he had to be desperate, she reminded herself. Still . . . "Nothing definite," she said shortly.

"Nothing definite! What kind of an answer is that?"

"It's the only answer I've got, Dad. Now please, leave me alone!" All at once, she was close to tears. Rather than give in to them, she launched her own attack. "And incidentally, thanks a lot for coming home and worrying Mom with this takeover business! Anna said that you talked about nothing else at dinner. You know the doctor said that we have to keep her calm."

His tone shifted to the defensive. "I didn't worry her, Rikki. I told her we have it under control—and believe me, we do. Young McCann is going to think he stuck his nose in a buzz saw before I'm done with him. But this is going to take up every minute of my time for the next two weeks or more—I had to tell your mother something. You know she knows me too well. She'd have gotten it out of me in no time, if I'd tried to hide it."

Even Rikki had to acknowledge the truth of this. "I suppose so . . . but we can't let it worry her."

"Of course not. And don't let it worry you." Her father hesitated, then added, "But Rikki, if you do hear anything that you think might help... Well, information is every-thing in this game."

Had her father ever really asked her for help before? Ever really needed her? And now that he should need her for this—to spy on Clay. Her throat tightened. "Dad, please don't ask me to— I—"

"Rikki?" he interrupted. "I'm sorry, but I have an ur-gent call on the other line. We'll talk tomorrow, all right?"

"Right..." Tomorrow, it had always been tomorrow that he'd promised to make time for her. But far too many to-morrows had come and gone.

Rikki went to bed shortly thereafter. Anxiety had driven out most of her pleasure, and she was not at all sure she was looking forward to her own particular tomorrow.

PERHAPS TO POSTPONE the day, Rikki slept late the next morning. Her father was long gone to the office, her moth-er's private nurse informed her cheerfully. And her mother was still sleeping. As for that poodle...

Rikki managed to wash her face, then throw on a pair of shorts and a T-shirt, in spite of "that poodle's" dancing as-sistance. Within minutes they were on the street, heading for Lexington Avenue. Purchasing a *Times*, a *Wall Street Jour-nal* and a coffee to go at a corner bakery, Rikki turned back toward Central Park, Foo pattering at her side.

Inside the park Rikki headed straight for her favorite tree. It was an old, old friend, one that she'd rediscovered in this last anxious month. Funny to think how much she had changed and grown over the years, and yet her tree had stayed just the same. It still had its smooth bark and the proper slant to its trunk for leaning against. Rikki settled into a patch of sunshine, unleashed the Foo, then looked around. Her tree was far enough from Fifth Avenue that the sounds of the city were magically muted. It crowned a small hillock, and from here you had a clear view in all direc-tions—no one could walk up on you unexpectedly. It was close enough to a well-traveled path to be safe, and far enough above it to offer privacy. It was the perfect place for thinking. Or for worrying. Leaning against the trunk she opened her paper.

The article she had hoped and prayed not to find was in the financial section of the *Times*. Its headline leaped out at her, and she sat straight. "VenturiCo bids $2.9 billion for U.S. Strategix."

VenturiCo was Clay's company, of course. With a little groan, she slumped against the tree and closed her eyes. So it was going to happen. It was not going to go away, no matter how much she wished it would. She groped beside her for her coffee cup, pulled off its lid and drank deeply. Then she looked again.

In smaller points below the headline, a sub-caption read: "Will Knife McCann slice up Strategix?"

Knife McCann...the name was all wrong for him. Clay wasn't some Wall Street cutthroat, butchering any company or person that stumbled across his path, as this article seemed to portray him. He was kind, caring...or at least he used to be. Remembering the way he'd looked at her once or twice the night before, Rikki shivered. She couldn't really claim to know him anymore, could she, after twelve years? He wasn't her carefree, handsome sailor in a white uniform anymore, that was sure. Clay had grown up. But how could he have grown into this—this Knife McCann? "No," she said aloud. He couldn't have. This was just some financial writer's romantic distortion of the facts. Like some overgrown boys' club, Wall Street adored nicknames. Clay's name had simply lent itself to that fierce abbreviation—that was all.

But if that was all, if Clay was still as kind and caring as he'd been twelve years ago, how could he be attacking her father's company? Her father had given him his start in the business world, after all.

She set the *Times* aside and reached again for her coffee. Then she remembered her charge. "Foo?" The poodle trotted around the tree and cocked her head inquiringly. "You stick around," Rikki warned her. She took a sip of coffee, then flipped through the *Wall Street Journal* till she found its corresponding story. "Takeover wizard strikes again!"

She groaned softly to herself. And it wasn't just Clay's treachery... She stopped, mentally erasing that ugly word. It wasn't just Clay's *ingratitude* toward her father that stung. What did that make Clay, that he should *want* to take over Strategix? How could he strive for the same goals, the same all-consuming and very male triumphs that her father did, and not be just like—The poodle took that moment to remind Rikki that she was here and needed entertaining. With a mock growl, Foo seized the strap of Rikki's sandal and worried it, shaking her head as she snarled with falsetto ferocity. "Off! Off! Gimme a break!" As if she didn't have troubles enough. Rikki shook herself free and stood. "Come on, then." They started down the hill to the footpath—a short jog would take the edge off this pipsqueak tyrant. And perhaps cheer her up, as well.

But why was she so blue? Rikki asked herself as she broke into a jog. Clay had kissed her last night—she should be dancing on air! She shuddered suddenly, remembering with every nerve in her body the feel of his mouth on hers, the hardness and warmth of his body as she pressed up against him. The incredible joy... To have felt like that last night, and now to be so sad...why? Had it anything to do with Clay at all? Perhaps this was simply worry about her mother, disguising itself as a free-floating depression.

Remembering her mother Rikki remembered her mother's pet. She glanced down, then around quickly. Far behind, a forlorn, tiny waif sat on the path. The Foo had a limited interest in jogging, and after that she expected to be carried. "You...bug-eyed fluffhead!" Rikki started back for her. It was time to head back to the apartment anyway. Her mother would surely be awake by now.

And Clay... Clay had said that he would call.

ELIZABETH CASEY was out on the terrace when Rikki returned. Holding Foo in her arms, Rikki paused just inside the open French doors. On the street below, the traffic murmured its endless song. Her mother lay on a chaise longue near the balustrade. As always, she had chosen the first place that the sun would find once it rose above the surrounding buildings. The top leaves of the Japanese maple were already tipped with golden light. With its branches quivering in the summer breeze, the tree seemed more alive than the motionless woman.

She's asleep—that's all, Rikki told herself as she fought down a familiar stab of panic. But, as she had done so many times in the past four weeks, Rikki felt compelled to make sure. Kicking off her sandals she stepped lightly across the cool, gray quarry tiles to stand beside the chaise longue.

Her mother's chest rose almost imperceptibly then sank again as she exhaled. Rikki breathed her own sigh of relief, then frowned as she looked down on her mother's pale face. Under the smudge of her lowered lashes, Elizabeth Casey's skin was disturbingly blue. She'd always had an aura of high-strung fragility, but nowadays she looked as if a strong breeze could snap her in half. *I'll let her sleep,* Rikki decided. It was all she could think to do for her. If there were only more she could do....

Glancing at the coffee table beside the chaise longue she saw that her mother had laid out her painting gear, had, in fact, started a painting. On the big block of watercolor paper, a wash of pale gray defined the highlights of the building across the street. Though the painting was barely begun, Rikki could tell from the faint pencil lines of the initial sketch that it would be lovely.

Elizabeth Casey had taken up painting about the time
Rikki left home for college. And though she still thought of
herself as an amateur, she was better than many profes-
sionals Rikki had seen. This summer, she had meant to ful-
fill a long-standing dream. She had planned to visit Europe
for three weeks, to paint castles and landscapes and since her
husband could not—would not?—find the time to go with
her, Rikki had promised to keep her company. But instead
of flying off on this adventure, Elizabeth Casey had nearly
embarked on another sort of journey altogether....

Rikki curled her fingers, fighting the urge to touch her
mother's face—an almost primitive need to assure herself
that she was really there. It was funny how you could grow
up, grow away...and yet when you came so close to losing
a parent, all your love came sweeping back, almost stunning you with its intensity. With her mother so ill and fragile, Rikki found herself fiercely protective. She had this
urgent need to see her mother happy, nowadays.

But perhaps that need was a selfish one. Perhaps, on some
level, a woman could never feel she had a chance at happiness, if her mother did not first achieve it. *You've got to
show me the way, Mom! It's not too late for that. I know it's
not.*

Rikki bent to examine the unfinished painting. The wash
was mat smooth, all its water evaporated. So her mother had
been sleeping for some time. She had so little energy.

Foo chose that moment to twist in Rikki's hands as she
tried to jump onto her mistress's lap. Juggling her in exasperated silence, Rikki retreated to the living room. "No, you
don't," she told the poodle as she tucked it under one arm.
"You're stuck with me for company today." And vice versa,
more was the pity. "Let's go find some breakfast."

Rikki was out at the library, choosing some books to help
her prepare for the courses she would be teaching in the fall,
when Clay finally called. "Did he leave a number where I
might reach him?" she asked Gretta Higgins, her mother's

morning nurse. He had called her! He really had called—somehow she had not really believed he would. She could have kissed the woman. She could have laughed out loud.

"No, dearie, I'm afraid he didn't. Sometimes men are as skittish as rabbits, aren't they?"

Rikki's smile widened to a grin—the image didn't fit Clay at all. Most likely he had called her between meetings or while he was out to lunch. He'd call again when he got a moment of quiet, surely.

But he didn't.

As the hours passed, the anticipatory butterflies in her stomach flew off to sunnier fields, one by one. The day seemed to darken and close in around her. Rikki fidgeted around the apartment all afternoon, and she found herself switching on unneeded lights as she wandered from room to room. She had a curriculum to write for the advanced biology course she'd be giving this fall, lessons to plan. She had plenty to do. Instead she found herself picking up books, putting them down, cleaning out a closet of clothes she hadn't worn since she'd gone off to college. And turning to scowl at the stubbornly silent telephone, or at the clock with its relentless hands. Her mother slept, woke to talk with Rikki and to paint for a little while and then slept again. The day dragged on, minute by silent minute.

Finally, after five, Rikki gave up. So that was that. Clay had fulfilled his promise—he had called. Apparently he'd felt under no obligation to call again. That had merely been one of those things men say at the end of a date. A graceful transition to let him walk out of her life as abruptly as he had reentered it. She ought to have been relieved. Ought to have been...

What she needed was a brisk walk—that was really what was wrong with her. She wasn't used to being penned in like this. This past month had been a strain, staying inside so much with her mother. How could she live like this, locked up in a box of stone? For even if that box had one of the finest addresses in the city, it was still a box. Suddenly Rikki had to get out. Now.

Her mother would probably stay in bed till supper time, which was always late at the Casey residence, in deference to her father's schedule. Though tonight Rikki doubted that her father would make an appearance no matter how late they held the meal. She had plenty of time for a walk. She changed her shorts for a pair of white linen slacks and a gray-green silk camp shirt that set off the color of her eyes. Perhaps dressing up would cheer her up.

As always, Foo and she headed around the corner and across Fifth Avenue to Central Park. The early evening promenade was in full swing by now. Usually this sight amused her. Today it only made her more lonely. That was one of the things she hated about the city—how alone you could feel in a crowd. You didn't expect people to speak to you. Everyone was so desperate for solitude that they all seemed to carry a little bubble of isolation around with them. Strangers didn't meet your eyes or smile in New York. Enclosed in her own little bubble of solitude, Rikki looked out dispassionately on the world around her.

Couples strolled home from midtown—the men with their ties comfortably loosened, the women in their elegant suits and their frumpy walking shoes, with their heels hidden away in their oversized purses or briefcases. Joggers panted past in sweat-soaked self-righteousness, their eyes turned inward as they listened to the "burn." On the green park benches that lined the paths, older people read papers, teenagers necked and bums snored, oblivious to the parade. Out on the grass, career women caught a few precious minutes of "quality time" with their toddlers, and Foo snarled at every one that dared to toddle toward her, thinking that here was the ultimate stuffed toy.

Rikki finally scooped her up before she changed one child's mind about puppies forever.

"Quite the guard dog you've got there."

Rikki spun around to find Clay standing beside her. "Oh!"

The sun had sunk to that special point in the sky, and everything was taking on a golden tone. The air itself seemed full of sunlight suddenly, as if they were both breathing gold. In this honeyed light, Clay's face looked as tanned as it had in his sailing years. And almost as happy. "Hello," he said softly. "Didn't mean to startle you." Like the other men in the park, he had loosened the knot in his burgundy tie. He held his suit jacket slung carelessly over one shoulder. But he didn't look like the other men to Rikki. He stood out as if he were haloed in gold.

"Well, you did!" You didn't expect anyone to speak to you when you were trapped in your little bubble of loneliness. But now, wonder of wonders, her bubble caught the sun, and spun off a rainbow of iridescent colors. Her bubble had expanded magically to hold two. Or rather three. Foo lifted her upper lip in a silent snarl, to show what she thought of this intrusion. "How did you find us?" she asked as Clay gravely offered his hand for Foo's inspection or delectation.

Foo chose to sniff—with ill-tempered deliberation—rather than nip. "Your doorman recognized me on the way into the building. He said I'd find you here." Clay stroked the poodle's topknot, and when that was accepted, pulled her silky ear. The dog's tail quivered ever so faintly. That settled, Clay looked at Rikki. "Want some company?"

Yours? Forever! "Please," she said softly.

They walked in silence for a while, their shoulders brushing too often, as if neither could walk a straight line. "Sorry I never phoned back," Clay said at last. "It was a crazy day."

"How's that?" It was so hard to picture him working. He belonged on a boat, his hands on the wheel, his eyes squinting toward the horizon. She couldn't see him cooped

up in an office, with phones and secretaries and paperwork.

"Nonstop meetings. Your father's lawyers started three
or four lawsuits against us today. Every time they filed another one, my lawyers would run tell me about it, then tell
me what they intended to do to counter the suit. And I had
a long interview—one of my public relations men persuaded a financial writer from *Forbes* to do a crash story on
my offer. It'll come out next week, and that's all to the
good..."

Good for you, Clay, but not for my father! Publicity was
crucial in the early days of a tender offer, Rikki knew.
Stockholders needed to be persuaded that the offer was a
serious one and a lucrative one. Clay could not buy control
of Strategix if its shareholders didn't offer him their stock
to buy. "I see..." she said unsteadily.

He glanced down at her. "Rik, are you sure you don't
mind?"

Mind? How could she help minding? Her father had
spent thirty years building Strategix, and now Clay pro-
posed to step in and take it away from him? She stooped to
put the Foo down, then stayed down, patting the dog, her
face hidden. Think of Mom! she reminded herself desperately. If Dad were retired, he could go to Europe with her.
They could buy that beach house out in the Hamptons that
she's always wanted. But still...

"Do you?" Clay insisted.

She looked up at him. "I'm having trouble with it," she
said frankly.

"Okay...so we won't talk about it." He took her hand
to help her back to her feet.

So we won't talk about it! Did he think that it would all
go away, if they just ignored it? Could he really be that cal-
lous, that insensitive? Still, as Rikki rose lightly to face
him—she stood almost under his chin—all her senses suddenly focused on the strength and warmth of his fingers, the

miracle of his touch. She had to tilt her head back to look up at him. His blue ocean eyes held a question, or was that an answer to some question of her own? She couldn't sustain his gaze long enough to find out. Turning away she walked on, or tried to.

He didn't let her go. Their arms stretched out, a warm and unbreakable link between them. Looking over her shoulder, she tried to smile, to make a joke of the moment, merely a friend's teasing, much as he had defused her advances when she was a child.

He shook his head with a kind of smiling wonder and followed.

Holding hands with Clay. Could she have died at some point without noticing it and gone to heaven? They strolled on wordlessly, their fingers entwined, their shoulders bumping. Children yelled in the distance, and somewhere beyond the trees a tenor poured out his heart in liquid, lyrical Italian. This being New York, that ravishing voice might have been a recording, might have been some star of the Metropolitan Opera, serenading them for the pure joy of it—just one more songbird, somewhat larger and more exotic than the park's regulars. Rikki could have burst into song herself.

"Ah," said Clay as they topped a hill. "My kind of place." He tugged her down the other side toward the lake.

"You must be a water sign," she teased. But it was her favorite place as well. On the nearby bank, a painter stepped back from a dreadful canvas to admire the full effect of a cobalt slash on his olive green water.

"Think that's supposed to be the rowboat out there?" Clay whispered in her ear.

She nodded, trying not to shiver, wishing his lips would touch her there again. And again. "How come you've never bought yourself a boat, Clay?" He could afford the boat he'd dreamed of now. Could afford a hundred of them. "Or have you?" Looking up at him, she saw his smile tighten

into something that was not really a smile. She'd seen that
look before—that time on the *Princess* when he'd cut his
hand. He'd smiled that way and denied the pain.

He shook his head, his eyes on the sunlit boulders,
smooth and gray as elephant backs, that rose above the water on the far bank of the lake. "No, I never have." His
hand squeezed her fingers almost painfully for a second then
relaxed again. "Guess I've been too busy for that."

So much for dreams. She hadn't wanted that answer.
Should have expected that answer. Life was all about
choices, wasn't it? Clay had clearly made his. And had left
his dream behind in the process. What had the *Wall Street
Journal* called him—a corporate raider renowned for his go-
for-the-jugular tactics? She shivered and tried to take her
hand away, but ignoring that, or perhaps not noticing the
gesture, Clay pulled her into motion again.

"I know—" He led her down the hill toward the boathouse. "Let's see if you still remember how to row. I had
enough trouble teaching you, that summer."

"Nonsense! I was a natural."

"Uh-huh, but a natural what?" Laughing at her indignation, he stopped by the kiosk that guarded the dock where
the rental boats waited. "Want to?" He nodded at the row-
boats.

She would have given her firstborn to row again with
Clay! Rikki glanced down at the poodle that had been trotting demurely by her side all this way. "But they'll never let
us take the Foo out. And it's getting late. My mother will be
worrying..." She hadn't told him yet about her mother's
illness, and somehow she did not want to right now.

"I can square the dog with the kid," Clay assured her,
meaning the boy in charge of the rental boats, who was now
eyeing them from the dock. "There ought to be a phone in
the Boathouse Café, over there. Why don't you call your
mother? Tell her you're in good hands and that I'll see you
home safely when you're ready?"

If Clay left it up to her, she would never go home, Rikki thought as she went to phone. But since that was not possible, she would steal an hour or two of sweetness.

It was the evening nurse who picked up the phone, however. "Your mother is having her first night out," she told Rikki exuberantly. "Your neighbor down the hall, that nice older lady—what's her name?—Mrs. Natwig? She invited your mother in for a light supper and a video that she'd rented."

"That's terrific—marvelous!" Rikki had wondered when her mother would find the courage to take this first step out of the apartment's safety. Had prayed that she would regain that courage.

"Your mother says you should come, too, when you get in. Only if you want to, that is."

"I don't think I can make it," Rikki said with no regret. Let her mother get an undiluted taste of independence. "If Mom gets in before I do, will you tell her I met a friend in the park? I'm not sure when I'll be back." She almost danced to the dock. Today was her lucky day, there was no doubt about it!

But when Clay tried to hand her into the stern of the dinghy, Rikki shook her head. "Oh, no! You were impugning my rowing back there. I'll show you."

"All right." With a grin, Clay settled into the stern. The Foo crouched beside him, peering over the side of the boat with white-rimmed, rolling eyes.

Rikki balanced her way to the center seat, while the boy steadied the boat. Clay's legs were so long that he'd had to tuck them under her seat. She straddled them gingerly and sat facing him. Her face suddenly warm, she bent over the oars, checking them with ostentatious care. Had she felt like this before, when he'd taught her to row? Surely not! What an innocent she'd been back then, and what an idiot now, to put herself in this position.

She looked up as the boy shoved the boat out into the pond to find that Clay was laughing silently at her. Cheeks burning, she laughed herself. It *was* ridiculous—and marvelous. Well, there was nothing for it now but to row. She dug in the oars.

Leaning back on the gunwale, his weight resting on his elbows, Clay watched, his eyes crinkled with amusement. The Foo decided that this was perhaps an entertainment rather than a disaster, and scrambled past Rikki, up to the bow. From there she leaned forward like a tiny, fluffy figurehead, her ears lifting in the faint breeze of their passage.

The trick was to concentrate on the oars. Feather them so that they angled smoothly into the water, rotate them slightly for the stroke, then lean into the pull. She must not think about Clay's well-muscled legs that she was practically sitting on top of, her own legs, spread wide and braced against the sides of the boat, the silky rushing feel of the water beneath them, the heat in her blood. Just think feather, dip, stroke, feather...

"You have the arms of a mermaid," Clay said huskily.

That was the same way he'd sounded last night in the elevator. Already humming along, her pulse accelerated. "Green and covered with scales, you mean?" Why couldn't she be serious with him? Somehow, this was too serious for her to take it seriously.

Clay's smile deepened slowly and he shook his head. No, that was not what he'd meant. Her eyes lingered on his smile, first fascinated, then trapped by it. His bottom lip was the wider, and beautifully carved. How would it be to kiss his mouth, to run her tongue along that generous curve, to tease him into opening to her? Last night had been too sudden, too unexpected for her to separate the sensations. If he kissed her again, would she dare to—

"Keep heading this direction, and it's going to be a short cruise, cap'n," Clay warned her.

Rikki glanced over her shoulder, then dug in one oar wildly. The boat pivoted in time, and they glided alongside, rather than into, the granite shore. "Whew!" she said on a laugh and could feel a blush rising again. Blast her fair complexion!

"Can't think of anyone I'd rather be shipwrecked with," Clay assured her wickedly.

But was he saying that just to be nice, or did he mean it? Rikki pondered that all the way down the lake, while the boat drew a silvery line through the duck-green water. Yesterday had been a chance meeting, but today... Today Clay had come looking for her, for nobody else... With that thought came a surge of joy that had to go somewhere. She dug in the oars to send the boat shooting ahead, then paused while they coasted along, her oars poised and uplifted like wings to either side. The silver drops of water raining back from them into the pool might have been diamonds falling around her. Into her heart. They were nearing a shore again, this one overhung with willows. The boat glided through the leafy, rustling curtain. Sunlight filtered into this tunnel, a private place of green and gold and dark waters.

"My turn," Clay said. He sat forward to put his warm hands over hers, stilling the oars in the water. They drifted, parallel with the bank, their hands and eyes joined.

"All...right." But had he meant his turn to row, or— His fingers tightened over hers, and he leaned forward. Half-mesmerized, Rikki found herself leaning forward to meet him.

"You're so damn kissable," he murmured ruefully and brushed her lips with his own.

By him, yes, she was kissable! Always had been, forever would be. Heat was flaming out from their lips, was washing up her wrists and arms from where his hands held her. Shuddering all over she leaned into him dizzily. Her hands clenched on the oars as if they might somehow anchor her

to this reality, while Clay's mouth spun her away to some
far-off, honeyed place of gold and softness.

Soft kiss, soft breath on her cheek, soft brush of his lips
back and forth through her eyelashes. He let her hands go
and plunged his fingers into her hair. "Oh, Rikki." His
fingers tightened, sending erotic little pains rippling across
her scalp. He tilted her head back and kissed her—not softly
at all this time. Someone was singing a little trilling cry of
wordless agreement, and she realized that it was her. She
laughed breathlessly as he tore his mouth away, arched her
neck for him as he pressed hot lips to her throat and then the
top of her shoulder. She shuddered, then laughed again.
Could this be happening? Was this what miracles felt like,
how joy tasted? How could she be so lucky?

Beep-beep! The sound was so alien that she opened her
eyes.

Beep-beep! It was a tiny, insistent sound, coming from
behind her.

"Damn!" Clay growled against her throat and let her go.
"It's my beeper, Rikki. Can you hand it to me?"

Beep-beep! Rikki whirled to find the source of the hate-
ful sound and dropped the oars as she did so. One of them
slipped out of its socket and slid into the water. "Oh!" She
turned back to grab it.

Beep-beep!

"I've got it. Just get me that beeper, Rik!" Clay caught
the oar and fitted it back into place.

Rikki turned again to find Foo pawing frantically at
Clay's jacket in the bow. *Beep-beep!* She grabbed the jacket
and passed it back to him. Clay snatched some sort of pa-
ger out of an inner pocket and jabbed its acknowledgment
button.

"Whew! That's better." He looked up with a grin.

"Yes." But it didn't feel better. She felt like an utter fool,
after that Chinese fire drill. How could she have let herself
go like that? Why, he could have done anything with her—

anything at all—right out here in the open. And he must realize that, mustn't he? She'd held no more of herself back than she had as a child all those years ago. All the flame that had been burning within her seemed to have risen to scorch her face.

"Rik," Clay said gently and touched her cheek.

God, if she could only believe that he wanted what she wanted! She didn't know what he wanted at all, did she? She looked away, breaking away from his touch and his gaze. "Your turn to row, Clay." If not quite steady, at least her voice was cool.

He spoke just when she'd decided he wouldn't. "All right." They exchanged places carefully. Clay picked up the oars, gave her a searching, rather ironic look, then feathered them delicately and plunged them into the dark water. He bent smoothly into his stroke, and the boat slid into sunlight.

What was he feeling right now? Amusement at how fiercely she'd responded to him? Or even...pity? She clenched her hands on the edge of her seat, then forced her fingers to relax, aware of what a giveaway they must be to Clay's sharp eyes. Think of something to say—anything. "What's the beeper for?" she asked, remembering it suddenly.

"That's my office. It means something important has come up, and I need to call them." He put his back into the strokes, the muscles of his thighs swelling as he pulled. The boat shot ahead.

Something important had come up... Something too important to be ignored in favor of a kiss. She could hear her father's voice again. *"Rikki. I have an urgent call on the other line."* Not a call from Rikki, but an *urgent* call...something that mattered. She shivered suddenly and found that her hands were clenched so tightly they hurt.

The oars squeaked as Clay shipped them, leaving the boat to drift in midlake. "Rikki." He leaned forward to capture her hands—held them prisoner between his own when she tried to pull away. "Rikki, look at me."

Something important had come up...and whatever it was, it had to do with the takeover of her father's corporation, she realized suddenly. Once again Rikki had that dizzying, sickening sensation that she stood on the wrong side of a gaping divide. *I should be there, not here!* But she was so undeniably here, with Clay's warm hands clasping hers.

"Look at me!" he demanded. When she did, his brows slanted in an expression that combined amusement with puzzlement. "Rik, I'm sorry if I went too fast back there. It's just that..." He hesitated, shrugged, then gave her his dazzling grin. Releasing her hands, he brought one of his own up to her face. A warm knuckle brushed her bottom lip, perhaps seeking her smile. Not finding it. "Well...that's why," he said roughly and picked up the oars.

As he rowed, Rikki turned to trail one hand in the water and kept her eyes fixed on the tiny wake that she made. The water was cold and nearly black now. No, Clay had not gone too fast, back there—it was not the speed with which they were proceeding that was scaring her. It was where she was going, and with whom!

CHAPTER FOUR

THE ROWBOAT nudged into something hard, and its bottom grated across gravel. Rikki looked up to find that Clay had beached them. But they were on the far side of the lake from the rental dock and the telephones.

"Don't worry." Clay answered her questioning look. "I arranged it with the kid. He'll pick it up later."

"But why?"

"My favorite restaurant's on the west side of the park. Besides, I don't like to backtrack."

He'd arranged it... Had he always been this certain of what he wanted? So ready to rearrange the world and its rules for his own pleasure? As Clay helped her out of the rowboat, she remembered the way he'd plucked her out of the midst of her parent's fight on the *Princess*—with no by-your-leave to anyone—and decided that he had been sure of himself. But back then he'd been her god. It had only seemed fitting that he'd acted with lordly assurance.

But now? Now Clay was expecting her to accompany him to his favorite restaurant, though he hadn't asked her if she was free, or if she wanted to. He'd even shown her father more consideration than that! At least he'd asked her father if he'd like to be vice president of their merged companies. But then, Clay had known that that invitation would be refused.

Just as he knows that you want to go with him. And if Clay was awfully sure of himself where she was concerned, it was only because she'd given him good reason to be. A spark of rebellion flared within her.

It flickered and went out as Clay smoothed a lock of hair back from her cheek, then tucked it behind her ear. "Hungry?"

"Famished, now that you mention it." And famished for touches of tenderness like that as well. Her eyes swam for a second. Fearing that he would notice even in the gathering twilight, she turned and called the Foo. Kneeling, she clipped the poodle's rhinestone leash onto its collar.

"That's not the kind of dog I would have pictured you with," Clay remarked as they walked toward the glow of the setting sun. "You need something with racier lines—an Afghan or an Irish setter to go with your hair. You're not the yappy little rhinestone type."

"Thank you," she said with heartfelt gratitude. "But this beast is Mom's." And yappy or not, Foo more than earned her keep. The little dog happily absorbed all the love and attention that her mistress's husband had no time for. And she gave all that devotion back in spades. *But I won't ever be like that, so lonely that I have to turn to a dog. I won't be!*

"What's the matter, Rik?"

"Oh...it just—just feels funny to walk in the park so late." And so it did, now that she thought of it. This was a first, to be out here after sundown.

Clay dropped an arm comfortably around her shoulders. "Not to worry."

Rikki fought the urge to shiver and to lean closer into his solid warmth. No, it wasn't muggers that would worry her tonight....

The restaurant was one she had never seen before on Columbus Avenue. As they approached it, Clay picked up the Foo. "Clay, we can't take her in there." It was a measure of Rikki's preoccupation that she hadn't thought of this.

"Sure we can." As they entered, the hostess hurried to meet them. Clay held the poodle out to her. "Terry, here's a paperweight for Virginia's office." While the cooing woman carried off an eagerly sniffing Foo, Clay led Rikki up the narrow stairs to a booth tucked into a corner of the upstairs gallery. From there they could look down through a carved and varnished balustrade to the busy bar below. Candles shimmered on the table, and a huge hanging pot of fuschia seemed to have been strategically placed to afford this booth maximum privacy.

"This is lovely," Rikki murmured while she admired the ornate, stamped tin ceiling overhead. "Did you call for a reservation?" Could he have been as sure of her as all that?

"Nope." Clay scanned the wine list. "This is my table. I hate to stand and wait."

It was a rare man who could toss off such an arrogant remark and make it sound charming. Did he ever do anything he didn't want to do? Or had his power taken him far beyond all that?

He reached some decision, closed the booklet with a snap and stood. "I'll have the waitress bring you a drink, Rik. Can you spare me a minute? My office . . ." He touched her nose lightly, waited until she nodded, then strode away.

Yes, his office . . . He was supposed to call in, wasn't he? Rikki looked down at her watch. It was nearly eight, and Clay was still thinking about work . . . And if he was, then it was because he wanted to. Not because he had to. She knew another man like that.

The waitress arrived with the wine and her menu just then, and Rikki fled gratefully from that thought. By the time Clay returned, his dark brows pulled together in a faint frown of concentration, she had perused the menu twice over. "This looks wonderful! I love California cuisine."

"Yes, Virginia can cook," Clay agreed as he topped her glass off, then filled his own. "The Cornish hen stuffed with

64 TENDER OFFER

jalapeño cornbread is superb. She uses a lime and honey glaze.''

"Virginia?"

His lips quirked for a second. "One of my acquisitions. She was vice president at Acton Tectonics."

Acton Tectonics—that was the last company Clay had taken over. Or maybe the one before that. Rikki looked down at her wineglass and swirled the liquid slowly. His acquisition...was that how he saw it? Did he think that he bought people as well as the corporations? But he'd never buy her father. Her father would sooner go down with his ship than be bought by Clay. Was that how this Virginia had felt?

"...she was getting bored with the business world," Clay was explaining. "So she used her golden parachute, and I threw in a little backing, and here's the result. And I get my own table."

A golden parachute—compensation money paid to executives laid off after a takeover. Her father didn't believe in golden parachutes. "Makes people too willing to surrender, if they win either way," she'd heard him say once. "You want people to go to the wall with you, then make darn sure they've got something to lose. The men at the Alamo didn't have parachutes!"

"As I live and breathe, it's Mac the Knife!" A heavy man in a business suit loomed up beside their table, a drink held at a precarious angle in one hand, his other hand extended. "I saw you come in, buddy."

"Bob..." Clay's smile was less than enthusiastic as he shook hands.

"McCann, you've got ice water in your veins! I don't know about this deal—taking on the Hard Case himself." Bob shook his head admiringly, and Rikki found herself studying the tablecloth. "That son of a gun's not gonna be easy. They say old Casey's got stainless steel—"

"Bob—" Clay cut in sharply. "I'd like you to meet Erika Casey." He shot her a look of exasperated concern as he completed the introduction. "Bob's an old business school buddy."

"Pleased to meet—" Bob stopped in mid-sentence, still holding her hand. "Casey? Not..."

"Yes." Bob's look of goggle-eyed dismay only increased her feeling that she was a traitor to be sitting here. Rikki disengaged her hand and tucked it into her lap.

Bob had turned back to Clay, his brow furrowed in comic confusion. "But I thought this was a hostile deal. What are you—"

"You know what they say about biz and pleasure," Clay reminded him. He wasn't frowning, but somehow the effect was the same.

"Don't mix'em," Bob supplied automatically. He still looked as if he were doing sums in his head.

"Exactly. And at the moment..." Clay lifted one eyebrow meaningfully.

Bob started, then backed away, his hands upraised. "Okay, okay, buddy! I can take hints with the best of 'em." He turned back to Rikki. "Ms. Casey, it's been a pleasure... Clay..." He shook his head at him, expressing a sort of awed admiration at Clay's imagined audacity. He turned, did a double take when he found himself face to face with the fuschia, ducked around it and was gone.

"Clown!" Clay muttered hotly under his breath. Reaching across the table, he captured both her hands. "Rikki, I'm sorry."

"It's all right." But was it? How could she feel so right, with his big hands enfolding hers, and yet...

"You realize that this *is* just business, my going after your father's company, don't you, Rik?" His thumbs caressed the tops of her hands while he searched her eyes. "It's nothing personal. I admire your father more than anyone I know."

"Admire him!"

"Absolutely. He got me into this life, you know. It was your dad who persuaded me I was wasting my time studying history that summer on the boat. I went back to college and switched majors in the fall."

No, she had never realized that. She tried to take back her hands, but he didn't let go.

"And then when I graduated from Harvard, it was your dad who gave me my first job. If anyone taught me the value of hard work, of setting a goal and then driving for it, it was John Casey."

Oh, God, did he think this would make her feel better? "I just don't understand you!" she whispered unhappily. "You admire my father. You say Dad taught you the value of hard work . . . but didn't he teach you anything about loyalty? How can you *do* this to him?"

"Ah-hem!" Their waitress stood beside them, a tray in her arms, a smile on her face. As Clay let Rikki go, she set two salads before them. "Virginia says not to order anything," she informed Clay. "She's playing with a new dish that she wants you to try tonight. Prawns—I can't figure out if it's Mexican with Thai influence or vice versa, but it smells wonderful."

"Fine." When she left, Clay turned back to Rikki. His face had not hardened so much as lost all its openness. "Things aren't always as simple as they seem, Rikki," he said evenly. "In business especially, a situation isn't just black or white—it's several shades of gray. Sometimes you have to balance one loyalty against another."

She pictured a gigantic balance scale, Clay's debt to her father in one pan of the balance, his duty to maximize his shareholders' profits in the other. Well, he'd made it clear which way *his* balance was tipping! In the candlelight, Clay's eyes were black mirrors, reflecting the flames, shutting her out. His lips formed a straight line, refusing to soften his philosophy by so much as a smile. He balanced his loyalties and made no apologies.

But, then, she was doing a balancing act herself, wasn't she? Rikki felt as if she were teetering along a tightrope, her arms widespread and reaching—even a smile, a touch at the wrong moment might send her spinning down into the abyss.

"Anyway," Clay said, interrupting her thoughts, "I promised I wouldn't bore you with business talk. So tell me about you. How did you get into teaching? The last time we talked, you were going to be a film director."

So now he chose to change the subject, did he? She wondered for a second if Clay might be less comfortable with his business philosophy than he claimed to be, then she rejected that hope. No, he simply wanted to hear about her now. "I wanted to be a director?" She smiled in spite of her worries. "I guess that was just a passing phase." So she told him about teaching science to ninth and tenth graders and gradually relaxed again. She told him about the funny parts of her job and the awful parts. About the time Henry Medeiros freed the dissection frogs.... The guinea pig named Darwin that she kept in the classroom as a reward—the daily top performer in each class got to cuddle him for the last ten minutes of the period. She might have even told Clay why she'd chosen teaching, but the main course came at that point. So they went on to other things, and she didn't tell him why. Didn't say that she'd chosen it in large part because she got her summers off. That she'd come to realize that this was her way of balancing her father's sad equation. Her way of saying that life should be balanced, that there was time for fun and laziness in life as well as hard work. Perhaps even time for love, some day... *But how can you have love without loyalty?* cried a small, bewildered voice somewhere deep inside her mind.

A hand rose up before her eyes. Rikki started, then sat without breathing while Clay's fingertip traced the arc of her brow, then feathered away. "Why the frown?" he asked quietly.

"I was frowning?" She couldn't think why. Couldn't think at all, at the moment. A touch could leave an echo behind it as a shout could in an empty room. Rikki sat motionless, savoring the echoes he'd set off within her.

When they'd finished their superb meal, Virginia came up for a visit. The chef proved to be a chubby, twinkling woman in a white apron, who plainly thought that Clay had hung the moon. She accepted their praise of the meal with complacent delight, then invited them to share a brandy with her.

Clay glanced at his watch. "I think tonight we'd better not, Virginia. Next time?"

"You know it." She soon bustled off with a cheery wave.

Foo was suspiciously fatter when the hostess brought her back to them at the door. And she seemed less than delighted to be leaving. Out on the street, Clay hailed a cab with his usual baffling ease, then glanced down at her. "Mind if we make one quick stop, Rikki?"

"Of course not."

They stopped only a few blocks away in the West Fifties. Clay drew a fingertip across her cheekbone. "One of my lawyer's junior partners lives here, Rik. It's pretty late. Mind waiting here in the cab a minute?"

She shook her head silently. A few minutes alone was just what she needed right now. For somehow, Clay's presence seemed to pull her off balance. In his company, she lost her sense of up and down, and she wasn't so sure she liked that sensation. It reminded her of some of the amusement park rides of her childhood—say, the Tilt-A-Whirl, that was it! Clay was a Tilt-A-Whirl. He whirled her off balance, reordering her life, effortlessly seizing the center of her world each time he entered it. And Rikki had always thought of herself as a Ferris wheel person. She liked to know where up was at all times. Or at least she'd thought that was how she liked it.

It was closer to ten minutes before Clay returned, carrying a tall stack of manila envelopes. She didn't have to ask what was inside them. Those papers meant work—more work—and it was now after ten. *But if he wants those papers tonight he probably means to work on them tonight.* That thought was as unpleasant as the first sickening swing of the Tilt-A-Whirl, but then it whirled away out of her mind. Clay got in beside her, and all her senses revolved around him.

As the cab pulled away, Clay picked up the Foo and tossed her gently to Rikki's far side. He put his arm around her shoulders to draw her closer. "How about a coffee and cognac at my place?" He felt her shiver and his arm tightened automatically. "Hmm?" He brushed his lips through her hair, then down to her temple.

She shuddered—fought down the urge to turn fully into his arms, wrap her arms around his waist and hug him fiercely. As if, if she could cling tightly enough, she might be able to squeeze out all the shadows that seemed to be rising between them. "I thought you said you didn't have time?"

"Did I?" His voice was husky, with just a hint of laughter. Warm and slow, his lips traced a path from her eyebrow to her cheek. "I just wanted you to myself, that was all."

And if she went back to his place, he would have her all to himself. Would have her all—there was no way she could, or would, resist him. *And he knows that!* she thought, as he tipped her head back to take a kiss. Lazy and sure and smiling, his mouth lingered upon hers. Time seemed to glide to a stop, then spin slowly around the warm, moving center of their desire. "Hmm?" Clay murmured against her lips.

Drowsily, dreamily, almost drugged with desire, she shook her head no. Lights flashed across her face, sparked in Clay's eyes for an instant as they passed under a theater marquee.

She felt his body go still for an instant, then harden subtly, his arms tensing, as if he were gathering strength to overcome this unexpected resistance. "Why not?"

Because she was a Ferris wheel woman, and he was a Tilt-A-Whirl. Because she was confused. Because, right now, no matter how overwhelmingly right it felt to be in his arms, the thought kept occurring, *We could never make this work. We'd make each other miserable.* But how could she say that, when she didn't know what Clay wanted?

Oh, he wanted her tonight, that was plain enough. His eyes were black with desire, and the hand at the nape of her neck kneaded her with a seductive, only half-conscious possessiveness. But for all she knew, Clay's desire for her was just a passing whim. She would feel like an utter fool, telling him that she feared they had no future, if he'd never even dreamed of one.

Clay bent his head again and put his lips to her ear. "A coffee..." The words were more kiss than sound. "A cognac..." His teeth found the lobe of her ear and nibbled ever so gently. She gasped and brought her hands up to his broad shoulders as if to push him away. Instead her fingers curled around the muscles there as if entranced by their warmth and hardness.

With a little breathless laugh, he leaned even closer, letting her feel all the heat and weight of him against her throbbing breasts. "And that's all," he promised, "unless you want more." The laughter shimmering just below the surface of his words told her that Clay knew what she wanted and would ask for.

"No..." She slid her arms all the way up around his neck. Their hearts were slamming together now, their breathing quick and shallow. "I . . . want . . . to go home."

For a long moment, he simply looked down at her, his brows pulled together in a half-bewildered, half-mocking frown. Then he shook his head. "You little liar. You're going to regret this as much as I will." But he kissed the tip of her nose, then turned his head toward their driver. "Make that East 71st, pal."

They rode in silence for several blocks, still wrapped together, Clay musing down at her face while the city lights danced and flickered across it. It was too dark to read his expression, but he seemed more amused than angry. Finally Rikki loosened her arm, leaned back against the seat and took a deep, shuddering breath. God, how she still wanted him! He stroked a skein of hair off her cheek, and without thinking, she turned to kiss his fingers. His hand paused for a very long moment, then dropped away.

"Rikki," he said simply, and his tone might have held tenderness, amusement . . . even pity. Or all of the above.

The taxi pulled to the curb beneath the awning that covered the entrance to her parents' co-op. The doorman opened the curbside door, and the Foo, recognizing home territory, let out a yap and bounded across them.

"Don't get out," she urged Clay. She needed time to think. There was no way she could think clearly around him, at all.

"Don't be silly." Clay spoke to the cabbie, then followed her into the building. He caught her arm just inside the door. "When do I see you again? Tomorrow for supper?"

She had to think. "I don't know, Clay . . ."

For the first time, Clay looked irritated. Frowning down at her, he caught her arms. "Now look, Rik—" Then, with a start, he stared over her shoulder. "Why, hello, sir."

Rikki whirled to find her father, ramrod straight in his gray business suit, his briefcase in hand, scowling at the two of them from where he stood by the elevator. The Foo lay at his feet, her front paws crossed stylishly.

"Evening." Casey's greeting sounded as if it had been measured to the last millimeter, clipped with precision, then tossed at Clay's polished shoes.

Still holding her arm as if she were a prisoner he'd taken, Clay started walking toward her father—it was not the direction Rikki would have chosen! He held out his hand. "Quite the fight your men put up today, sir. That third suit had us sweating for a while."

Her father stared down at Clay's hand. Finally, almost as if it rose in spite of his will, his own came up to meet it. "That was just the preliminaries, McCann. The real campaign starts tomorrow."

Clay's hand tensed on Rikki's arm. "Oh?"

Her father's face was etched deeply with lines of exhaustion. As she watched, it hardened into what might have passed for a smile, and Rikki remembered what Clay's friend had called him that evening. The Hard Case. "Ten o'clock tomorrow. We tender for *your* company, McCann. Sixty-two dollars a share."

Clay didn't move, except for his fingers. Rikki almost cried out, but that punishing contraction had gentled before she could protest. "Won't do you much good, sir," he said evenly. "We're allowed to buy you one day before you can buy us. Once I control you, I'll have one day to cancel your tender offer."

"By the time you're my age, McCann, I hope you'll have learned that there's many a slip..."

"Twixt cup and lip." Clay completed the proverb with a smile, but it never quite reached his eyes. "Quite true, sir, but then...that cuts both ways." The two men stood motionless, their eyes locked, and Rikki was struck by the electricity of the confrontation—it was as if a bolt of raw energy rebounded between them. Then Clay shrugged and turned to Rikki. "Dinner tomorrow," he declared. "I'll call you to set a time."

Beyond his shoulder, she could see her father's face turning scarlet. She could feel the blood rushing to her own cheeks. The arrogance of this man, to address her like this before her own father. Clay might not have taken over

Strategix yet, but he acted as if he'd bought a controlling interest in *her* stock!

"I don't think so," she said coldly, her chin lifting a notch.

But his hand came up to her jaw, cupped it to tilt her face higher. Her mouth dropped at this outrageous audacity, and then Clay was half laughing against her lips. "Then think *again*," he told her. He kissed her as if he had all the time in the world and no audience, then he stood looking down at her for an instant, returning her glare with a faint, crooked smile. He moved her aside gently, turned to nod at her father. "Evening, sir." And he left them, his strides long and jaunty as he went out to his waiting cab.

CHAPTER FIVE

IN RIKKI'S BEDROOM the morning light filtered greenly
through the wisteria vine that draped down from the terrace above to overhang her windows. Sitting at her dressing
table Rikki brushed her hair and waited for the sound of the
front door closing. She was not leaving her room until her
father left for work.

They had not talked at all last night. After Clay had made
his exit, she had been too outraged to trust her own voice.
Ignoring her father's reproachful glare—as if she'd invited
that kiss somehow!—she had taken the Foo out for a visit
to the nearest tree. She'd stayed outside until her father gave
up and went upstairs without her. For she had no intention
of discussing that kiss with anyone... except perhaps its
perpetrator.

Pausing in her brushing she rubbed the back of one hand
across her lips, a slow, half-conscious, totally sensual gesture that ended abruptly as she met her own eyes in the
dressing room mirror. Damn Clay, anyway! How could he
have done that to her? For that kiss had had nothing to do
with her and him, and everything to do with her father. That
kiss had been a challenge. *Think I can't take your company?* it had said. *I can take your company and your
daughter, as well. Just watch me.*

Well, she would not be the rope in their stupid tug of war
game—she would not be! Swinging away from her own
stormy face, she slammed the brush across the room. It hit
the pillow on her bed with an unsatisfying thump. Drawing

her bare feet up onto the tapestry-covered seat, she crossed her arms around her legs and sat there, her chin on her knees, her hair sweeping her shins. Shutting her eyes, she shut out the feel of that final mortifying kiss and concentrated instead on the ones that had come before that in the taxi. Remembering them, she hugged herself harder. Those kisses had been for her, surely. The way he had simply looked at her in the cab, their eyes trading secrets while the city lights swept over them, surely he'd been thinking only of her at that point.

Clay couldn't have, wouldn't have, used her just to psych out her father, would he? Psychological gamesmanship and one-upmanship were standard tactics in a takeover blitz-krieg, she understood that, but Clay wouldn't have used her that way...surely? Could that have been his aim for the last two days in seeing her? His sole aim?

"No!" she whispered aloud. *No, I know you, Clay. Not as well as I wish I did. Not as well as I could, if you gave me the chance, but...no.* No, he wouldn't use her that way. No, that last kiss in front of her father had simply been an impulse. Outrageous, impudent, but not quite unforgivable. Not quite...

Her head lifted as she heard the front door close quietly. She glanced at the old-fashioned brass alarm clock by her bedside. 7:30. Her father had stayed late—hoping to talk with her, no doubt. By now his temper would have cooled as well, and he would be wondering if she'd learned anything useful from Clay last night. She shook her head and uncurled herself slowly. *No way, Dad. I'm not going to betray either of you.*

When Rikki stepped onto the terrace a short while later, she found her mother already there. Lying on the chaise longue, Elizabeth Casey held her poodle curled in her lap. Her head drooped back against the chair's cushions, and her eyes were closed.

She was only asleep, Rikki told herself as she stopped beside the chair to peer down at her mother anxiously.

The poodle stirred, then lifted her head, and her mother opened her eyes. "Oh, Rikki..."

"Morning, Mom." Thankfully, Rikki stooped to kiss her cheek and to inhale the faint smell of roses that for her would always evoke her mother. "You're up early." She straightened to look around for a chair, found one and brought it over by the chaise longue. Studying her mother's face she made a conscious decision not to frown. But she didn't look good this morning—the shadows were even deeper under her eyes than usual. "Didn't you sleep well?"

"No, not too well... Your father woke me when he came in last night... and then I couldn't get back to sleep." She smiled, making light of the matter. "I got so tired of lying there with my mind going round that I finally got up and painted." She nodded at the watercoloring block on the coffee table.

Rikki picked up the block. The painting was a study in grays and deep purples, layer on layer building up a boulder-like mass.

"Other way round," her mother told her with a laugh.

"Oh." Rikki rotated the block, and slowly, her father's face coalesced out of the shadows.

"He's usually a restless sleeper," Elizabeth Casey said. She leaned forward to study her work. "But he was so tired last night, he didn't move once. There's just enough light that reflects in from the terrace..."

"It's beautiful," Rikki said softly. He looked so much younger asleep, or was it just that her mother painted him through memory's loving eyes? Or perhaps this was her mother's way of reshaping reality to her own desires—Rikki had never seen him look so vulnerable. She glanced at her mother. *Her* guard was down all the way, while she gazed at her husband's face. As it had been down when she painted this portrait. "But you should have been sleeping yourself, Mom. This is no way to get your strength back."

"I'm fine," Elizabeth Casey insisted, her eyes still fixed on the watercolor. "It's your father I'm worried about. This takeover..."

This was what Rikki had feared. The takeover was doubtless the cause of the insomnia. "You can't let it worry you," she said carefully. "Dad can take care of himself. Besides..." She hesitated, then voiced her treachery. "Did you ever wonder what might happen if Dad did lose control of Strategix? He's never going to retire willingly, Mom. But if he was forceably retired...well, who knows? A lot of good might come of it in the long run. He'd have to find something else to do." She half smiled at the absurdity of the idea. "Maybe he'd take up a hobby. Something you two could share. I know you've always wanted to travel."

Her mother sat back abruptly, her hands steadying the poodle as it nearly fell from her lap. "Is that what you're hoping will happen?" There was a note of condemnation in her voice that her daughter had not heard since she was a child.

Rikki found herself blushing. "It might be the best thing that *could* happen."

Her mother shook her head emphatically. She started to speak, then stopped herself as if she didn't dare to yet. Half defiant, half ashamed, Rikki waited for the rebuke. But gradually, her mother's lips softened, and the tension between the women eased. "I used to dream of something like this happening, Rikki, back in the years when you were growing up," she admitted finally. "Even prayed for it."

Yes, Rikki could remember those years all too clearly. Her mother had fought for her husband's time in those years. Had even won a battle once in a blue moon. But at what cost to all of them?

Elizabeth Casey picked up the sleepy poodle and held it like a baby at her shoulder, her fingers combing through its fur. "Do you remember," she said dreamily, "the time I went to Seattle for a few months, to that watercolor workshop? It was your second year in college, I believe." When Rikki nodded, she went on. "There was really a workshop, of course, but that was also a trial separation."

"Mom!" Rikki had been astounded that her mother would leave her father for such a length of time, but that it had been a spiritual as well as a physical distancing had never even crossed her mind.

"I was hoping that John would miss me enough...he could have retired a wealthy man even then, of course..." Her mother's eyes were fastened on some distant point, and her hand stroked the poodle hypnotically. "But finally, I began to realize that he would have followed me if he could have. There was no one else, if that's what you're thinking. But there was the business. And somehow, finally it came to me that John could no more walk away from his business than he could walk away from his own heart, Rikki. He *is* Strategix. McCann doesn't understand that. To lose the company would be as if someone tore out his heart." Her eyes sharpened, returned to the present and swung back to her daughter. "And so I came home..."

Rikki felt as if someone had taken the picture of her life, shredded it and politely handed her the pieces. Something would have to be reassembled from the jumble, but at the moment...

"And so that's why I'm so frightened now," her mother continued quietly. "Losing Strategix would destroy your father."

In her old picture of the world her father had been the strong one. Rikki shook her head. "Mom, that's ridiculous! Why Dad's as tough as...as tough as a Sherman tank." *As tough as I thought you were fragile.* And yet she'd been here by choice all along... Here, not because she could imagine no other place, but by her own choosing. "Even if he should lose, he'll just get up and start over again."

"I hope so..." The poodle was squirming, and her mother put her down. "But even if he did..." Her hands found each other. The fingers entwined, then whitened as they clenched. "If you think he works hard now... I don't know if you remember how it was when you were very young, all his traveling, the hours he kept, the anxiety when he'd take another big gamble..."

"Oh, yes, I remember..." She'd been a child, dreaming wishful, foolish dreams that any good could come out of Clay's attack. Her mother was right—her father would not change, if he hadn't changed by now. If Clay beat him, he'd not retire to a new and delightful existence. He'd be more likely to work himself half to death. Just when his wife needed him the most, he would be effectively gone from her life for a period of years.

"Please don't worry, Mom. It's not going to happen, anyway. Dad's an old warhorse when it comes to corporate infighting. He'll make Clay McCann wish he'd never been born, before he's done with him. Just wait and see."

"And that's another thing I've been worrying about." She touched her daughter's arm. "You and Clay..."

The Foo reared up against Rikki's chair. Rikki picked the dog up and blew in her ear. That earned her an indignant yap and a midair snap, as she knew it would. "That you don't have to worry about. It's a non-issue, Mom," she said briskly. She ruffled the poodle's coat, then set her down on the tiles. "I got over my crush on Clay years ago."

"But you went out with him the night before last."

So her father had not told her of last night's fiasco yet. "Only 'cause Dad pushed me into it. He had some ridiculous notion that I could play Mata Hari. Find out all Clay's secret strategies." She forced a smile, dismissing the topic, and stood. "I just did it to humor Dad, that was all. Now, I guess it's time I walked this beast, if Gretta's come in yet. Could I bring you an o.j. before we go?"

On the way down to street level, Rikki ignored the poodle frisking around her feet. What was she going to do? Things would only get tenser and tenser for the next two weeks, as the day for execution of Clay's tender offer drew nearer. How could she hope to shield her mother from her own fears? Blast Clay anyway for picking on her family! There were a thousand other companies he could have gone after—why had he chosen her father's?

Out on the sidewalk, she and Foo turned away from the park. She would get coffee first, then drink it under her tree while she tried to think. There must be something she could do.

A car door slammed behind her. "Rikki!"

She stopped short and looked to see Clay striding away from a cab that had been double-parked across the street. The cab pulled away and her heart turned over—one slow cartwheel. Clay... She found a smile of greeting spreading across her face and smothered it instantly. She was supposed to be angry, after all. But that wasn't the way she felt... It was all she could do not to run to meet him.

He was covering the ground fast enough for two of them, anyway. "I thought you told me you walked that mutt at eight?" he growled as he loomed up beside her.

Well, *he* was having no trouble not smiling this morning. Her own impulse in that direction died instantly. "I guess we got a late start."

"I've been waiting here since eight."

What was she supposed to do, apologize? If anyone owed anyone an apology... Her resentment eased, however, as she stared up at him. "Clay, are you ill?" His face was so fine drawn as to be almost haggard, his eyes faintly bloodshot. His usual splendid carriage was even more erect than usual, but stiffer, as if he carried himself with a conscious effort.

He managed a smile. "Nope. I just missed a few hours of sleep last night. That's all." Taking her arm he started her down the street. "This is the way you were heading?"

She nodded. So he had not slept well, either. She'd had a miserable night herself, after the way they'd parted. "What time did you get to sleep?"

"About five. We brainstormed all night, deciding how we were going to respond to your father's offer today."

Rikki's smile vanished. So he had not lain awake, agonizing about their relationship, as she had done. His concern had been all for his business. She thought about love, while he thought of ways to destroy her father!

"I'd be fine, except that this is the second night in a row I've done without. Then there's the reason I wanted to see you this morning. I can't make it to supper tonight."

"I don't believe we had a date," she said coldly. To the east, the sun edged above the soft morning clouds, sending a shaft of light sweeping down the street. It struck them full in the face. The harsher light threw Clay's face into brutal contrast. It carved the lines of fatigue deeper into his cheeks, showed the jut of the bones beneath his skin. For an instant she saw him as he would look at fifty—leaner, tougher, with the same air of command as her— *No.* Rikki swallowed hard, and looked away.

"Don't you?" He swung her around to face him. Dropping his hands on her shoulders he smiled at her.

It wasn't just that he was acting like her father, devoting night and day to business, he even *looked* like her father... Or no, he didn't really, but there was something about him...something of that same indomitable spirit. What *was* there in a woman that attracted her to that unbreakable hardness, when it was that hardness that would ultimately break her? Her father had never swerved one inch from his chosen path to accommodate her mother. And now she was choosing such a man herself? A man whose heart belonged to his balance sheet and his appointment calendar? *No, oh no.* Never...

"Rik?" Clay touched her lips, an oddly tentative gesture for him. "You with me?"

No, she could never be.

"Rikki?"

She blinked, focused on his quizzical face and flushed. But, then, he hadn't asked her to be with him, at least, not for more than an evening, had he? He wanted her father's corporation on a permanent basis, but who knew what his plans for her were? "Of course."

He studied her for a minute, watching the color rise in her cheeks. His lips twitched. "You're not still mad about last night, are you?" A taxi pulled up beside them and beeped its horn. Still holding her gaze, Clay lifted one hand in acknowledgment. "My cab," he explained. "I had him circle the block." His hand came up again to trace the line of her jaw, then it slid around the nape of her neck to hold her. "About last night... I don't know what to say. Anything that feels that right... I'd be a liar if I said I was sorry." He gave a shrug.

"Even if it made me angry?"

His grin was breaking into view, tired looking, but still beautiful to her eyes. "When you're angry, you light up like a Roman candle—all sparks and color. I've only seen it once or twice, but it's wonderful. I want to see it again." His voice roughened. "I want to see all of you, Rikki."

She shut her eyes and shook her head.

A car horn honked.

"Damn, we're holding up traffic here. And I've got a conference in twenty minutes." Clay pulled her forward. "I'll call you tomorrow."

No. But his lips were on hers already, and she was responding, softening, curving in to mold herself against him. *Oh, no. I don't want to feel like this!* But even as she denied the emotion that was roaring down upon her, it swept over her like a breaking wave, and she rose on tiptoe to meet him.

Fingers spread wide, his hands slid slowly, sensuously down her back. Then, with a sudden violence that forced a gasp from her, Clay hooked an arm around her waist, shaping her to his overarching body. Claiming her.

No, I don't want to feel like this! But she did. Twin suns seemed to be rising in her breasts where they flattened against his chest . . . another sun burned in her belly. Her fingertips dug greedily into his hard shoulders, though she would have fallen if Clay had let her go. But he wouldn't, she thought exultantly. He wouldn't now.

Somewhere a car horn was honking, and someone was cheering raucously. "Yeah! Way to go, buddy!"

Clay groaned against her mouth, a laughing, rueful sound, then tore his lips away. Blocked by his taxi, three cars were honking now. Reluctantly, slowly, his arm loosened and he let her down off tiptoe.

Oh, don't! She no longer knew what she was protesting, knew only that he mustn't let her go.

But he did. "I'll call you," he promised and backed away.

Don't. She swallowed and tried to smile. Even returned his wave as his cab roared into motion. Numbly, she turned to watch it go. She didn't see the indignant glare aimed at her by the driver of the first car to follow Clay's taxi, nor hear the cheerful howl as the second driver blew her a kiss and drove past. Her eyes were only for Clay.

But Clay did not look back. By the end of the block, his head was bent over something he held in his lap. His briefcase, no doubt.

No, THERE WAS no way. No way it could work out. To continue seeing Clay was to go running to meet a devastating heartbreak—it made about as much sense as playing blindfold in rush-hour traffic on Fifth Avenue. He was everything she'd ever sworn to avoid.

And everything she'd ever wanted.

Slumping against the brownstone on the corner Rikki looked up at the street sign. East 53rd—good Lord, how had she walked this far? And how could she want him—a man

who might very well destroy her father? A man who...who
might even be trying to use her as a weapon against her father?

"No." Realizing she'd spoken aloud, she started and
looked around her. But people who talked to themselves
were a common sight in the city. None of the passersby
spared her a glance. No, surely Clay had no designs on her
in that way. He'd never tried to pump her for information,
never asked her to spy as her father had done.

But no matter what his intentions were, she had to stop
seeing him. There was no way it could work out.

Claws scrabbled against her bare calf. She glanced down
to find a panting and bug-eyed Foo reared against her leg.
"Sorry, shortstuff. Did I walk your poor little feet off?" She
picked up the poodle and settling her into the crook of one
arm, turned back uptown. Her mother would be wondering where they'd gotten to.

She had to stop seeing him... But how could a decision
that was so right, hurt so much? It was the right decision,
surely, to stop this before it had really started?

Aren't you about twelve years too late? she mocked herself bitterly.

Yes... Well, she had gotten over Clay once before. She
would just have to do it again.

*Sure. All you do is wait—and hurt like hell. For about
four years!* But better that than living lonely for a whole
lifetime as her mother had done. No, she would not love a
man like her father. She would not.

IT WAS ONE THING to resolve not to see Clay again and another to tell him. For once Rikki opted for the coward's
way—avoid him, until he forgot her. As busy as Clay obviously was, that shouldn't take long. Or so she would have
thought.

"Your young man is on the phone," Gretta announced as she met Rikki at the front door on the following day. "Again."

"Oh." It was the third time he'd called. The first two times this morning she had been out with the Foo, trying to walk away her blues. Rikki set the books she had just bought for her mother on the hall table. "Did you tell him I was out?"

"No. I told him I thought I heard your key in the lock. He's on the line."

Her breath caught in her throat. So all she had to do to stop this aching was run to the phone, pick it up, speak . . . She balled her hands into fists, then let the breath escape in an inaudible sigh. "Well, would you . . . tell him that it wasn't me, that I'm still out, please, Gretta?" She met the older woman's eyes with difficulty.

"Ahh, it's like that, is it?" The nurse shook her head. "You sure look like you're in to me."

"Well, look again!" Rikki flared. She swung open the door and stepped back into the hallway. She didn't quite slam it behind her. *Oh, God.* Hugging herself hard, she leaned against the corridor wall. Why did it have to hurt so?

The trick was to stay busy. But that would have been easier at her own home. In Rhode Island she would have been able to fight this pain by seeking out women friends, by burying herself in preparations for the coming school year, by concentrating on any one of a hundred chores or decorating projects around her apartment. *I want to go home,* she admitted and closed her eyes. She wanted to go home and hide there like a wounded animal until this pain stopped.

But she couldn't go home, she reminded herself. Not yet. Not until her mother had regained her self-confidence. Not while she was worrying so about Clay's attack on her husband.

Clay . . . Rikki opened her eyes wide and gulped a deep breath. The trick was to stay busy. As busy as Clay was keeping, apparently. His name and his picture were everywhere—the Strategix-VenturiCo takeover war had even made it to the front page of the *Times* this morning. And the *Wall Street Journal* had run a picture of Clay, smiling, side by side with one of her father wearing his suffer-no-fools scowl for the camera. The article had said that twenty percent of Strategix shareholders had offered their stock to Clay already. He couldn't buy it for another twelve days, but it was there in the tender pool, waiting for him. Things looked grim for her father. If shareholder sentiment kept running that way, Strategix didn't have a prayer.

Worse yet, her mother had insisted on seeing the papers this morning. She'd read every word of the two articles, then had gone white-faced to lie down in her room, saying she had a headache. But she just had to stop worrying about this! Rikki had hurried out to buy her some light reading and even a joke book in the hopes that—

The door opened beside her. "It's safe to come in now," Gretta announced, then marched away.

But was it safe to stay in? Clay called again, around four-thirty. At least this time it was the evening nurse who answered the phone. Rikki looked up from the book she had been reading aloud to her mother. "Would you please tell him I'm out right now, Miss Warner?" She looked down at the book again without meeting her mother's eyes. Where had she been? The words blurred before her and none of them made any sense. Nothing made sense...

"That was Clay?" her mother asked gently. "Don't you want to..."

Rikki shook her head. "No, I don't, Mom." She flipped backward one page angrily. Where had she stopped reading?

"Is it...because of your father?"

Because of loyalty to him, did she mean? Well, that was part of it. And the other part had to do with her father, as well.

"Yes," Rikki said simply.

"I see..." Her mother considered her for a moment, frowning, then nodded and patted her knee. "Maybe that is wise, darling. Perhaps later..." She sighed and leaned back in her wingback chair.

Later? Once Clay had swallowed Strategix? Her father's corporation would easily double the size of Clay's holdings. If Clay was a workaholic now, how would he be once he'd doubled his responsibilities? To say nothing of the fact that her father would never forgive him. Rikki shut the book with a snap and stood. "I think I'll walk the Foo now."

"Hi, stranger." Rikki padded into the kitchen.

Hand on the refrigerator door, her father turned. "You're up late."

"I heard you come in." She tightened the belt on her bathrobe. "Have you eaten yet?" It was past eleven, but that meant nothing with her father.

"Had something around five," he said vaguely. He looked toward the living room. "Your mother?"

"She went to bed hours ago. Now sit down, and I'll warm you up some stroganoff."

He was exhausted. The force of personality that normally surrounded him like an aura was all turned inward tonight. His face was gray and set, his shoulders held rigidly square. Dutifully, he sat at the counter.

His docility tugged at her heart. Somehow, much as she pitied him, he was easier to love like this. She found herself almost smiling as she prepared a plate of leftovers for the microwave. Face it, she liked doing things for him. Switching on the oven, she stood staring at the revolving plate of food for a moment. Was this all her mother had ever wanted, to have him here to care for? How did the song go, "How can I love you if you're not around?" She sighed. This was the first time she'd seen him herself, since Clay had kissed her under his nose two nights ago. *Don't even think about that!* "Milk, Dad?"

He nodded. "How's it going?" she asked as she poured him a glassful.

He shook his head. "Not good. We've been looking for a white knight, in case worse comes to worst, but no luck so far. No one wants to cross McCann."

Her father must be desperate indeed if he was considering selling Strategix to a friendly company, a white knight, that would agree to buy under more acceptable terms than Clay was offering. "I'm sorry," she said as she brought him his leftovers.

He shrugged. "Don't be. We're not licked yet." He speared a bite, then sat there, fork poised. "If we could just find his partner..."

"Whose? Clay's?"

Her father nodded. "He's got a silent partner, Rikki, I'm sure of it. He can't use our jet engine division—it's almost identical to his own aeronautics division. The government will hit him with an antitrust suit for sure, if he tries to hang on to that. So he's got to have someone waiting to buy it off him. If I could find that partner, offer him a better deal than McCann means to give him..." He turned to her, and she saw it coming.

"No, Dad." She slid off her stool.

"Rikki, all I need is a name. McCann has to be in close touch with this man, to keep him up to date with daily developments. I've got my people watching VenturiCo headquarters, but McCann's security is airtight. And there's a copter pad on his roof, so we can't—"

"Dad, please. I've told you... Besides, I'm not seeing him anymore."

"Why not?"

"Why *not*? Because of this! Because of you! Because—"

"Rikki?" Her mother stood in the doorway, swaying slightly, her eyes heavy with sleep. "What's the matter?"

"He wants me to— He wants me—" She shook her head in frustration as the tears filled her eyes. "Oh—ask him!" She slipped past her mother and headed for her bedroom. *Clay, why did you do this to us?*

THE NEXT DAY was another day of waiting and worry. On her morning walk with the Foo, Rikki kept expecting— hoping?—to turn and find Clay striding after her. No such luck.

Not wanting to bring the newspapers into the apartment where her mother would see them, Rikki read them in the park. Things looked grim for her father. Twenty-five per cent of Strategix stock had been tendered to Knife McCann by now. And her father's countertender was not doing so well. Perhaps the VenturiCo shareholders thought his countertender was just a bluff meant to scare off Clay, and that he really could not hope to buy Clay's company.

When she returned, Gretta reported that Clay had called—twice. "Sounded like a long-distance call to me," she added. "And he didn't sound so happy."

Well, that made two of them.

She was eating lunch with her mother on the terrace when the phone rang again. Rikki put her glass down slowly and looked toward the open doors to the living room. The ringing stopped as Gretta answered the phone.

"Clay?" her mother asked.

Rikki shrugged. Who else? When was he going to take the hint?

"Perhaps... you should talk to him," Elizabeth Casey suggested. "Your father seems to think that you might be able to—"

"Oh, Mother, not you too!" Rikki bit her lip. "I'm sorry, I didn't mean to snap like that, it's just—"

"Phone for you, Rikki," Gretta announced.

"I'm *out*, Gretta. How out do I have to get? Would you like me to hang off the railing, would that be out enough to—"

"It's a young lady." Gretta turned with majestic dignity and disappeared.

Was there one person in the world who wasn't mad at her? Didn't want something from her? Just one?

There was. "Rikki!" Samantha Boswell's warm, laughing voice bubbled down the phone line. "Since it seems you're never coming home could you use a visitor down there?"

"You? Oh, please!"

There was a silence from the Massachusetts end of the line. "That bad, huh?" Sam said after a moment. "Your mother?"

"No, it's not that... Well, yes it is, partly. I can't—when do you get here?"

"Day after tomorrow, if you're available." Sam had to come to town for a conference with a client on Monday, she explained. If Rikki had time, she would come down the day before for a visit and some museum hopping.

"That would be terrific—wonderful!" Rikki had not realized until then just how much she was missing her own life, her own people, these last few weeks of caring for her mother. She hung up the phone with the greatest reluctance.

That was the high point of her day. After lunch a delivery boy arrived with some groceries and—the real purpose of the order that her mother had placed—copies of the *Times* and the *Wall Street Journal*. So much for Rikki's efforts at censorship! Rikki watched in worried silence while her mother read the latest on the takeover duel. Halfway through the last article she dropped the paper. "So it's really going to happen," she said quietly. "John *is* going to lose." She leaned back in her chair, her eyes wide, then slowly her hand crept to her breast.

"Mom?"

"I feel . . . funny," she whispered. "My pills . . ."

Fighting down panic Rikki scrabbled in the pocket of her mother's robe for her ever-present pills. She fumbled open the cap, gave her one, then raced to the kitchen to find Gretta.

The nurse took it all with almost maddening calm. Mrs. Casey needed to lie down, to relax and stop worrying, that was all. "And don't you go fussing her," she warned Rikki. "The last thing she needs is to start worrying that she's having another heart attack. Her heart just gave a little hiccup, that's all. It could happen to anybody. Now stop hovering and dithering, would you?" She shooed Rikki out of the bedroom.

That was easy for her to say. It wasn't her mother, after all. Rikki spent the rest of the afternoon alternately pacing the terrace and trying to read, while her mother slept.

Gretta had just come to the door to tell her good-bye for the day when the phone rang. "Might be the doctor again." She disappeared inside, but was back in a moment. "Nope, it's Mr. You Know Who. He says, and I quote, 'Cut out the nonsense and come to the damn phone'."

So... Rikki took a deep breath. He'd taken the gloves off. He wasn't going to politely accept her hint and go away. Well, she could be as stubborn as he was, especially after this. Her mother's heart would not be "hiccuping," if it weren't for this man. "Tell him I said no." She bit it off precisely.

Gretta shrugged. "He's not going to like that."

No doubt. But apparently he accepted it. That was the last time Clay tried to reach her, and the day ended in ominous quiet.

The next day was worse. It was one thing to live dreading, and yet anticipating, a confrontation. To live knowing that there would be none, that Clay had accepted her rejec-

tion and moved on, was infinitely worse. All the colors
seemed to have bled out of her world.

The only bright spot was that her mother seemed no
worse. Not much better, but at least she was up and moving around again. And today she did not contrive to read the
papers.

That afternoon Anna Wiley was coming for tea and a
visit. Knowing her mother would be well looked after, Rikki
seized the chance to escape. She felt as if she were suffocat-
ing inside the apartment.

If she'd been in Rhode Island it would have been easier.
She'd have taken her depression outside. Miles and miles of
walking on a windy beach might have blown the blues out
of her heart and her head, helped her to start putting this
behind her. But in the city there were no soothing beaches.
Instead, Rikki fled to the streets.

She spent the afternoon walking, window shopping,
browsing through bookstores. It would have been a delightful day, if she'd had someone to share it. By herself the
pleasures were... downright dreary. But this was how you
did it. You just kept living and moving and staying interested, and before long it didn't hurt anymore. So they
said...

As dusk fell she stepped off a bus and walked the last
block to her parents' co-op. She met Nurse Warner trotting
down the street, an anxious frown on her chubby face.
"Miss Warner! Is my mother—What are you doing down
here?"

"Oh, Rikki! Your mother's poodle—you didn't see her
come this way?"

"Foo?" Rikki stared aghast at the leash dangling from
the woman's hand. "You've lost the Foo?"

Miss Warner lapsed into a confused and self-excusing
babble. The gist of it seemed to be that Anna was still with
Rikki's mother and that the Foo had grown restless. Nurse
Warner had offered to walk her. But the Foo had not been

cooperative when shown the nearest tree. The doorman had observed that Rikki often let her off the leash while she did her duty, and so Nurse Warner had tried that. She'd been chatting with the doorman, had only taken her eyes off the Foo for a second, but when she'd looked down again...

"Which way did she go?" Rikki demanded. If her mother lost her pet on top of all else...

"I don't know. She just vanished." The nurse started to repeat her theory of how this disaster had come to pass, but Rikki cut her short.

"I'll look for her. But you stay downstairs till I get back. I don't want Mom to find out she's gone. She'd die!" Cursing herself for that choice of words, Rikki set off at a run.

She usually walked Foo before dark in the park. It was her fault that this had happened, expecting that Foo could wait an extra hour for her. The little prima donna! There was no way she could have crossed Fifth Avenue alone. Rikki paused at the corner, scanning the avenue for a white, crumpled little body. The traffic roared past. Some of the cars had switched on their lights. The traffic light changed at the corner of East 72nd street, and for a moment the pavement was bare. Free of cars and free of small crushed animals. Could Foo have seized such a moment to make it safely across?

Rikki had to wait for the next change of lights to make the dash herself. *If I was a poodle, where would I go?* That was simple enough. Foo would probably follow their usual late-afternoon stroll, taking the path north toward Conservatory Pond and the statue of the Mad Hatter's tea party.

But it wasn't late afternoon now. Rikki hesitated at the entrance to the park. Her eyes swept the deserted path until it curved out of sight, and she found herself sniffing the air. She smelled only damp earth, mown grass and auto exhaust from the avenue behind her. What had she expected to smell—danger?

Don't be silly! She wouldn't be going deep into the park, after all, and it wasn't that late. The danger was to her mother, if Rikki came back without that moronic poodle. Taking a deep breath, she stepped through the gateway.

CHAPTER SIX

THE PARK TREES arched overhead. Beneath them she could still see, but the light had an underwater gloom to it, drowning all color but the deepest shades of green and purple. Muted by the intervening leaves the traffic on Fifth sounded like a river rushing in the distance. That sound faded as she moved down the pathway.

"Foo?" She could have called aloud, but somehow she didn't want to. Within this shadow world, there might be other things to hear her besides the poodle.

The path curved out of sight, with no small pattering white shape to break its dark monotony. Her heels sounded too loud in the stillness. "Foo?" She should turn back. This wasn't wise. But by morning Foo might have wandered off anywhere. And her mother—

From somewhere ahead a high-pitched yip sounded. "Foo!" Rikki threw all caution to the wind. "Foo-Foo-Foo-*Foo*?" As she called, she broke into a run.

The yip sounded again, then turned into a series of squeaking, shrill barks, growing ever more frantic as she approached. Mingled with the dog's frightened yelps were the sounds of laughter now—boys' or—Rikki stopped short—could they be men? The poodle burst into view—barking hysterically as it came. Charging along at her heels stumbled three teenagers. They were laughing too hard to chase the dog efficiently. Leaning down to grab at her the front runner tripped and went sprawling, and the other boys whooped and vaulted over him. One drew alongside the tiring dog.

"Foo!"

The poodle let out a squeaking snarl and made a final sprint. A fluffy white cannonball, she closed the last few feet between them, then leaped. Rikki didn't even stoop. Foo landed in her hands, a tiny, heaving, trembling weight. From the shelter of Rikki's arms she whirled around to berate her tormentors. Her bark was almost an octave lower now that she thought she was safe.

But was she?

The boys staggered to a halt before them. "Hey, that's our dog!" one of them panted. He reached out for Foo.

Rikki stepped backward. "Sorry, but she isn't. She's my mother's dog. Her name is Foo."

That cracked them up again. "Foo-foo," the middle one jeered incredulously. They were changing their stance, though, as they caught their breath. The two flanking their spokesman fanned out, so that they stood slightly to either side of her. All of them were grinning.

Against her palm she could feel Foo's heart beat, at a rate too swift for counting, a continuous vibrato of terror. As if in pursuit of the poodle's, her own heart started slamming, the blood thumping its echo against her eardrums. These were just kids! she told herself. As a teacher, she ought to be able to handle kids. But these were like none she had ever faced in a suburban classroom. They might be only fifteen or sixteen, but there was something about their eyes... And they were taller than she was.

"Well, she's ours now," claimed the middle one. "Finders keepers." He grabbed for the dog.

With a falsetto snarl and a flash of teeth, Foo lunged to meet him.

"*Yeeoww!*" Flinching, he squeezed his fingers and cursed savagely. "Bite me, will you? I'll *kill* you, you little rat."

"Don't!" Rikki retreated another step, and the boys to her sides moved with her like basketball guards. "Look, I'm sorry, but you're scaring her."

Foo belied that statement with another series of contemptuous barks.

Rikki raised her voice slightly, trying to keep it friendly. "You did find her, though, so I certainly owe you a reward." But she'd left her purse with Miss Warner, at the co-op. "So if you'd like to come back with us to my apartment..."

"Huh!" the boy to her left grunted. That sound contained a world of broken promises.

The leader's attention had shifted from the poodle to Rikki and as his eyes roamed over her, he started to smirk. "Got me a better idea."

Oh, no. Rikki swallowed, and her hands clenched on the Foo so tightly that the dog whimpered.

"Why don't you come with us, baby?"

"All right!" crowed one of the others.

"No!" She took a step backward, trying to draw the breath to scream, and they caught her arms above the elbows. She should scream, but there was no air in her lungs and if her heart beat any faster, she would die here and now.

"Hey!"

That shout came from behind her. The kids swung around, swinging her with them.

Walking through the twilight, Clay McCann moved toward them. He approached smoothly, without hurry, utterly silent after that first yell.

Rikki had seen dogs fight on the streets of the city. His approach reminded her of that—murderous intention was clear in every line of his body, the menace like a shock wave extending before him.

She found she could breathe again.

"Uh oh..." one of the boys muttered at her ear.

The other one shifted his feet. "Maybe we—"

Suddenly they both moved. Heaving Rikki into Clay's path they took to their heels. Still clutching the poodle she staggered, twisted a heel, tripped over her feet, then warm hands closed around her, pulling her into blessed safety. Clay's arms wrapped around her, crushing her to his chest. "God, Rikki!"

Squashed between them the poodle squealed, and Rikki laughed wordlessly—it sounded more like a sob. As he hugged her again, she burrowed her face into his shoulder, inhaling his safe, beloved scent. Tonight there was a hint of sweat, something indescribably masculine overlying the usual smell of him and his body throbbed stove-hot against her cheek. He'd been running.

"You little idiot!" He caught the poodle, pulled her out from between them and dropped her at their feet. Foo reared against their legs, begging to be picked up again. Clay ignored her. Still pressing Rikki's head into his shoulder, he stared down the path over her head.

"They're gone?" she murmured and shuddered all over.

"For now." He pulled her away from him to where he could see her face. "You idiot." Yanking her up on tiptoe he kissed her with a violence that took her breath away. His arm locked around her ribs, straining her to him until she thought her ribs might crack. "Nut!" He kissed her eyes, her nose, her cheeks and returned to her mouth. "What the hell did you think you were—" His lips traced an angry, burning hot trail down her throat to the hollow at its base.

Her pulse was still thundering—fear merged with passion without missing a beat. She shuddered and arched against him, giving herself completely to his hands and his lips. As his hand cupped her breast, she cried aloud, a soft cry of exultation.

The sound seemed to rouse him. His head came up, though he stil held her, the stroke of his thumb fanning her into shivering acquiescence. His eyes unreadable in the darkness, Clay looked down at her for an endless moment, then at last bent his head to her breast. Warm lips nuzzled, sought, then found the throbbing center of all sensation. His teeth closed on her delicately through the silk of her blouse. She cried again, a single, wondering sound, and molded herself against him from knees to waist. He groaned deep in his throat, kissed her breast and let her down off her toes.

If Clay had asked, she would have sunk to the grass by the path there and then. He didn't. Breathing heavily he stared down at her through the darkness. Then he hooked an arm around her waist. "Let's get out of here."

He hurried her along the path. The Foo trotted beside them, almost underfoot, occasionally leaping at her leg in a plea to be carried. But Rikki had other things to think about, or to try not to think about. If Clay hadn't come along... "How—how did you find me?"

"I was coming to see you—meant to drag you out of your castle kicking and screaming if I had to. But your doorman stopped me. He told me what was up and where he thought you'd headed. He was getting worried, and he sure worried me. I ran, made a guess which way you'd gone... But if I hadn't heard the dog..." His arm tightened around her until she gasped. "Idiot!"

Reaction was setting in. She felt as if her body were spiraling around a dark core of emotion. First it had been terror, then passion and now it began to feel like...like anger—he was hustling her along almost faster than she could walk. Or perhaps it was frustration. Whatever it was, the emotion had to go somewhere. She needed to vent it somehow, lash out at something big and solid enough to take it. She saw herself hitting him, wrestling him, falling beneath him, glorying in the overwhelming hardness and strength of him. Making that wonderful strength her own. He pulled her to a halt at the park entrance.

For the first time, by the lights of the passing cars, she could see him clearly. Clay looked as she felt, with her adrenaline still surging—dangerous, aroused, spoiling for a fight or a tussle. "Come home with me." It was more statement than question.

The poodle bounced against her thigh. "I can't, Clay. I've got to take Foo back to my mother."

"We'll give her to the doorman. He owes me one for letting you go off on your own like that."

"He was inside, and anyway, he didn't *let* me go. I went." What did he think she was—a child? Still?

"More fool you. Now let's dump the dog and go."

"No." What was she doing? What had happened to all her resolutions concerning Clay? Nothing had changed, except that now she owed him her life. That realization brought a rush of emotion with it. How was she to pay that debt, except by giving him her life? And she couldn't do that—there were good reasons she couldn't do that. She'd spent three days, brooding over those reasons until she was almost ill with it all. While he—he'd been out playing her father's game, building his stupid empire.

"No?" He frowned down at her. "Why not?"

What monumental conceit the man had. He wasn't inviting her out for dinner or a cup of coffee, he plainly meant to take her home to his bed. Did it ever enter his mind that she might not want to come? That she did—fiercely—want to go with him only fanned the flames of her anger. "Because I don't want to!" she cried passionately. "What do you think I've been trying to tell you, the last few days?"

"That's just what I meant to find out." Clay looked around. To their left was a place Rikki had always loved. A monument—shrine, actually—to Richard Morris Hunt, a shell-shaped little amphitheater built into the outer side of the park wall. Stone benches curved out to either side of the bust of the great man, forming a secluded nook where one could sit and look out on the avenue and yet be sheltered from all views except the front. Clay steered her to it, heedless of the resistance in her steps. Dropping onto a bench, he pulled her down beside him. "Why the hell have you been avoiding my phone calls?"

"Because I didn't want to talk to you." And she didn't want to now. She didn't want to talk—she wanted to run, to hit out ... to squeeze him tight in her arms.

"Why not?" As if he read her need for flight, Clay half turned to brace an arm on the wall past her, hemming her in. Their chests were nearly touching.

"Why not? You should know why not!"

"Because of this takeover? Rik, this is an even match—you don't have to side with your father."

"Who else do you expect me to side with—you? He gave you your start in business, you claim to admire him, and now you're trying to destroy him?"

"I'm trying to buy his company." Clay's voice was exaggeratedly patient, but its undertone was ironic. "That's not quite the same thing as destroying a man, Rikki. Companies are bought and sold every day of the week. Sometimes the deals are friendly, sometimes they're not."

"It may be just business to you, but Strategix is everything to Dad, and you know it! How can you do this to him?"

He sighed, looked away from her and swore softly. When he swung back, his eyes didn't waver. "That's the way the game is played, Rik. If you haven't noticed, business is concerned with winning, with profits. It's not about taking care of your fellow man." His words were bitterly ironic, but she couldn't tell which of them he was mocking; and she didn't care.

"Then the rules stink!"

"Maybe they do," he agreed. "But while I play the game, I'm going to play it as hard and as well as I can. Your father would understand that. That's the only way I can play it."

And that was the plain, unvarnished truth of the matter. She had never seen him do anything by halves on the *Prin-*

cess, once he set his mind on something. She doubted if he knew another way to approach life.

The Foo leaped onto the bench beside them and pawed at Rikki's thigh with sharp claws. She endured this, her mind whirling around the inside of the trap that held her. "Your father is going to be just fine," Clay continued with quiet conviction. "He's a heck of a lot tougher than you're giving him credit for. And don't forget he's tendered for my company now." He scooped up the poodle and set her back on the ground. "Would you be happier if I lose?"

Would she? "But you won't," she said bitterly.

His face showed a kind of wry satisfaction as he nodded. "No, I won't. I don't lose, when I want something enough."

And were they discussing a corporation, or herself, or both? Not that it mattered anymore.

Clay lifted a lock of hair off her shoulder, rubbed it between his thumb and forefinger. "So that's what's been bothering you... Is that all?" He tucked the curl behind her ear, then his hand lingered.

Was that all! She ducked away from his touch, as far as his other arm would allow. Wasn't that quite enough?

"Is that all?" Clay repeated, but he didn't try to touch her again.

What more did he want? Well, he could have more, if he wanted it! "No, there's my mother—you're wrecking her health. I can't stop her from worrying about this takeover and how it will affect Dad. She's had one heart attack already, this summer—why did you think I was visiting for so long? And if she has another—" Suddenly, Rikki's face was wet with tears, but she didn't sob—she would *not* sob. She leaned her head against the wall and glared up at him.

"Rik..." Clay raised a hand to her face, then withdrew it as she flinched. His voice was painfully gentle. "Rik, I didn't know..."

"And now that you do?"

They stared at each other, both frozen. It was the ultimate test. If he cared enough to spare her mother, then perhaps...just perhaps...

But slowly, Clay shook his head. "It's too late to turn back now, Rikki." He let out his breath in a frustrated hiss. "Can't you— Could you take her away someplace? Until it's over?"

"It's over." His words echoed inside her head, two simple little words, but heartbreaking in their finality. They cut off all hope, all chance of happiness. Desolately Rikki shook her head. "I asked her to come stay with me at my place in Rhode island, or maybe to go out to Anna Wiley's estate in Southampton." Angrily, she reached up to swipe a tear off her nose. "She won't. She says Dad needs her."

Clay caught her tone of disbelief. "Maybe he does," he said quietly.

"I can't think what for. He's worked till almost midnight every night since you started this. He's gone before she wakes up in the mornings. How could he need a woman he never takes the time to be around? How could any man?"

"Still," Clay insisted. He reached up to wipe her cheeks dry with his palm, ignoring the way she squirmed beneath his hand.

"Still your takeover may kill her," she told him when he'd finished. "Just as it's half killing my father—and what did he ever do to you? Why did you have to pick on him?"

"Why shouldn't I? He had what I wanted. His plastics division is the best in the world. And I need it."

His cynicism stole her breath away. How could he have changed so? Or had she ever really known him at all? Utterly defeated, she simply sat. There was nothing left to say.

But if she could not think, she could still feel. The heat of his body radiated out at her, enveloping her as surely as if their bodies had been stripped naked and pressed together. God, she was so hot. So tired. So sad....

"Is that all?" Clay asked again.

"Is that all?" Sadness switched back to rage with a vengeance. Was he discounting everything she'd said? Mocking her? She had no more words to express her frustration. She would have slapped him, but he was too close. Instead she threw up a hand between them and tried to shove him aside.

He caught it and held it trapped against his chest with an ease that only doubled her outrage. "Fine. And now I'll tell *you* something, Rikki. This isn't you talking tonight—it's the fear talking. You had a nasty scare back there."

"You don't know me at all, if you think this is just fear talking." A great wave of loneliness swept through her, not driving out the rage, but overlaying it with pain. If Clay didn't know her, who did? She thumped his chest with her other hand, and he caught that as well.

"I know you very well, Erika Casey, and I mean to know you better." Clay gathered both her wrists into one hand against his chest, then framed her face with his other. They stared at each other for an immeasurable time, she with chin lifted defiantly, he seemingly on the brink of a smile.

If he smiled while he held her helpless like this, she would never forgive him. Never.

He didn't. "Right now, you need a hot bath and a hot toddy." His words were husky and soothing, as warm as the fingers that idly fanned her cheek.

She shuddered. "That's all you think I need?" *You don't know me at all, then.*

"No, it isn't," he soothed. "You need to be loved within an inch of your life. Till there's not one thought in your mind...till you're so soft and warm and drowsy that all you can do is smile and go to sleep. And when you wake up...well..." At last his grin crept wickedly into view. "I'll still be there." Lifting her hands to his mouth he kissed her fingertips. "When you're ready for that, Rikki, come see me. In the meantime—" He stood, with an abruptness that startled her out of her trance. "Let's get you home."

Clay held her hand while he led her and the Foo across the avenue. Rikki let him—couldn't do otherwise, anyway—and she was too far away to care. Her mind was reliving his words, turning them to shadowy images that intertwined and interlaced to a soundtrack of muffled heartbeats. She was so hot, so tired, so sad. So wanting...

A few feet from her parents' co-op, Clay pulled her to a halt. Within the lighted lobby, she could see the doorman and Miss Warner, peering anxiously out at her. She would have to rally to face them, somehow. Have to find a final word for Clay. Reluctantly she turned to face him. "Thank you," she said quietly.

"For? Oh..." He shrugged, looking almost boyish in his embarrassment. "I'm just sorry I couldn't bash them for you. But I didn't want to leave you."

Oh, Clay. Don't leave me. Oh, don't! But his fingers released her. "Goodbye," she said, and it sounded like a death knell.

He wouldn't have it. His lips quirked. "Till whenever, Rik. You know where to find me." *And what for!* his dancing eyes reminded her.

"Sure. At your rotten, damned office—day or night!" She had a sudden, vivid vision of them making wildly passionate love upon his desk. He'd have an enormous one, no doubt.

Clay threw back his head and laughed. "Only too true, for the next week or so." Hooking a knuckle under her chin he tilted her face up for his kiss. "Till then," he murmured. "And don't be too long!" He turned and left her.

If she'd had a weapon, or even a word left, she'd have hurled it after him. He was at the corner, his hand uplifted toward some invisibly approaching taxi, when she turned and went inside.

CHAPTER SEVEN

"POTATO KNISH today, dumpling figure tomorrow," Rikki murmured as she studied the sign listing the pastries available at Zabar's takeout counter.

"Lord, you're in a rotten mood," Samantha Boswell declared. "Look at it this way—if it hadn't been for a certain guy last night, you'd have probably never eaten another knish in your life. You ought to eat two of them just to celebrate." She gave Rikki a little push. "Go grab us a table and I'll get the food. You're obviously not fit to choose."

Sam was being overly optimistic as usual. On a Sunday their hopes of a table in Zabar's were nonexistent. The few small tables and the counter along the wall were already packed with customers. There was hardly room enough to spread a *New York Times* in here, much less swing a cup of coffee, though plenty of people were trying.

While she waited near the door, Rikki mulled over Sam's innocent choice of words. *Not fit to choose . . .* And yet she had. She'd chosen not to go with Clay. Chosen to send him away . . . What if Sam were right?

Across the deli, Sam reached the head of the line and placed her order. Rikki's friend was in no danger of turning into a dumpling herself. Although she was built to rounder lines than Rikki's fine-boned slimness, the lawyer's curves were attracting plenty of attention from the man in line behind her, Rikki noticed. The girl back of the counter had to speak to him a second time before he realized it was his turn to order.

Outside the deli, they settled on a bench placed on the median between the uptown and downtown lanes of Broadway. It was early yet and the traffic was light. Somewhere a church bell tolled. Freed from their weekday rat race people strolled in ones and twos, walking their dogs or searching for their Sunday morning bagels and lox, the *Times* and some fresh air before the temperature soared. From her paper bag Sam produced two steaming knishes, looking like well-browned hockey pucks, and two cardboard cups of capuccino. "Only in New York," she murmured reverently.

That was easy enough to say, or feel, when she didn't have to live here. If Rikki had to be anywhere, and she supposed she must, she would have rather been sitting two hundred miles to the north, in her own apartment that overlooked Narragansett Bay.

Or in Clay's place, wherever that might be. She could have been there... They would have been waking about now, she thought, her eyes stinging. To wake with Clay on a Sunday morning... To have coffee and cuddling in bed, then to stroll in the sunshine, hand in hand, to find breakfast as that lucky young couple across the street was doing. She bit too far into the soft, buttery dough of her potato-mushroom knish and burned her mouth. "Ow!"

"Mmm," agreed Sam, "dangerous, but heavenly. Sounds like this man of yours. Knife McCann—I love it."

"I wish you'd be serious about this, Sam." Rikki was beginning to regret that she'd told Sam her problems. Frowning, she blew on the cinnamon-speckled cream that floated on top of her coffee. She ventured a cautious sip.

"I'm sorry, Rik. I'm just trying to counterbalance your gloom and doom. Can it really be that awful, to have a rich, sexy man chasing after you? I mean, I should have such problems!"

Rikki sighed. "I'd like to know how you'd *solve* such problems. He's going to win, Sam. The financial analysts all say so, the Strategix stockholders obviously think so, and you just have to look at him to see that he knows he'll win. How can I love a man who's going to ruin my father?''

Sam licked a dab of whipped cream off her lips, then frowned at the cup she held. ''I wonder...if...you aren't taking this all wrong, Rik—this takeover struggle. You're looking at this like a woman.''

''Not too surprising,'' Rikki said dryly.

With a rueful little grimace Sam nodded. ''But men don't see it the same way we do. They don't take business personally. That's why I had such a hard time making it in corporate law at first, do you remember? I'd spend all day fighting a lawyer on the opposing team in some deal. We'd go at it hammer and tongs from nine to five—no holds barred, eyeball to eyeball, nobody giving an inch. If I made one legal slip, my opponent would cut me off at the knees! By the time we'd settled the deal and signed the papers, whether I'd lost or won, I'd *hate* the son of a gun. But at the end of the day that son of a gun would look at his watch, give me an altogether different kind of smile and say—'' she lowered her voice to an ingratiatingly seductive bass ''—can I buy you a drink?''

The mixture of indignation and incredulity with which Sam showed herself receiving this invitation was irresistible. Rikki found herself laughing. Sam laughed herself, then took a quick sip of her capucino. ''The first time one of the guys pulled that on me, I nearly hauled off and popped him one in the chops—I kid you not! But by the second or third or fourth time it happened, I started to realize—they were sincere. They really wanted to pal around with me in the evenings—it wasn't just some cynical scheme to pick my brains about a deal or to gain unfair influence through fraternization.'' She finished her coffee and put the cup down. ''It's just that they held no hard feelings. Men...don't...*take it personally*. What happens in the conference room is totally separated from what happens in the bar—or the bedroom—later on. They don't mix business and pleasure."

Clay had said just that, hadn't he? Still...

Sam inspected the half knish that Rikki had abandoned and finally tore a piece off it. "The best example of male-think I know is pro football. Have you ever watched them on TV, where you can see them close up? When the play starts, those cadillac-sized hunks will do their level best to flatten the other team. You watch them in action and you figure you're seeing fractures, concussions and general maimings all over the field. Then the ref blows his whistle, the play's over, and they laugh and help each other up out of the dirt! It's just a game to them." She popped the piece of knish, with which she'd been gesturing, into her mouth.

"So what you're saying," Rikki said slowly, "is that whatever Clay is doing to my father, he's doing without malice."

"Exactly." Sam licked her fingertips with catlike daintiness.

"But if he destroys my father, even in an oh, so impersonal way?"

Sam gave her a look that combined sympathy with an insider's cynicism. She held out her hands, palm up. "I don't know what to tell you. It's the way of the world, Rik. Their world—the business world. They made it, and they play by their own rules. The same rules your father has been playing by for the past thirty years."

"And I *hate* that world!" Rikki said with a vehemence that shocked even herself. "I hate it—I'd never marry anyone from that world!"

Giving up all pretence Sam appropriated the last of Rikki's knish. "Do you think that's what he's after—marriage?"

Rikki sighed. "I don't know... Probably not. He certainly hasn't said." She closed her eyes for a second, remembering the touch of his fingers on her cheek with an almost physical longing. "It doesn't matter, anyway. I wouldn't marry him if he begged."

"Sick, sick!" Sam muttered. She looked contrite when Rikki scowled at her. "Sorry, but...look, I know what it has always been like with your father, the way he's neglected you and your mother. But just because Clay is also in business, it doesn't necessarily follow that he's a raving workaholic, does it?"

She'd asked herself that, about a thousand times at last count. "He's chief executive officer of a Fortune 500 company, Sam."

"Well...could he have inherited the position?"

Rikki laughed without amusement. "Hardly. His father was a grocer up in New London. No, Clay did this all by himself, and he's not thirty-five yet. You know what that means."

Sam nodded and looked less cheerful. "But maybe, after this deal, he'll be ready to slow down," she said stubbornly.

Rikki gathered their trash and jammed it into the bag. "You know how many times I've heard my mother beg my father to slow down?"

"But Clay's not your father," Sam pointed out. "You're taking all your hurt from the past and dumping it on Clay's head. Are you sure that's fair?"

She didn't know what was fair, anymore. All she knew was that she hurt—so much that she could not sit still. Rikki shrugged and stood. "Well, let's not let him spoil today, anyway. What'll it be—the Met, or the Museum of Modern Art?" She lobbed the bag of garbage into a city trash can— or tried to. It missed. With a sigh she walked over to retrieve it. It was going to be that kind of day. Or maybe...that kind of life.

THAT EVENING they ate Chinese takeout on the terrace with Rikki's mother. Rikki returned from the kitchen with the reheated egg rolls to find her mother picking her friend's brains.

"There's only one way I can think of that your husband might win, Mrs. Casey." Sam shot Rikki a glance that plainly said *It's not my fault!* and turned back to her hostess. "After announcing a tender offer, a company has to wait fifteen days before buying—that's the law."

Rikki's mother was sitting forward in her chair, her hands clenched together.

"Your husband started his bite-back offer for VenturiCo one day later, so he won't be able to buy control of McCann's company in time to stop him. But . . ."

Rikki sniffed and put down the egg rolls on the table between them. "These will get cold if we don't eat them."

"But," Sam continued, now too caught up in her train of thought to take the hint, "the fifteen-day rule changes, if a second company tenders for Strategix. That turns the clock back for McCann! McCann wouldn't be able to buy until ten days *after* the second tender was made. That means—"

"That means that, in the meantime, John would be able to take control of VenturiCo!" Elizabeth Casey exclaimed. Clapping her hands, she looked almost girlish in her excitement. "That must be what John is up to."

"Dad's out of town," Rikki explained. "He's been making a tour of all Strategix's divisions with the chairman of—"

"Wait!" Sam put up a hand. "Rikki, I don't want to know who your father is courting to be his white knight. That kind of information is absolute dynamite. If McCann got a whiff of it—"

"As if you'd tell!"

"Of course I wouldn't, but I'd rather not know. Tomorrow I'll be sitting down to a conference with twelve people or so downtown. I'd be scared the facts might seep out of my pores."

"That's all right," Elizabeth Casey intervened. "What matters is that John still has a chance."

But how good a chance was it? Rikki wondered as she served her mother some sweet and sour shrimp. What had Clay said last night? *I don't lose, when I want something enough.* And when he said that, he had not been talking only about Strategix. Remembering the look in his eyes, she shivered. He was so sure of himself. So damn sure. And yet he hadn't tried to win her today. There had been no phone calls for her while she'd been out with Sam. *But then, he expects me to come to him, next time...* She could feel his desire pulling her, pulling... She was the meteor fleeing across the night sky, and he the dark planet, pulling, pulling, gravity all on his side. Their collision wasn't a matter of *if*, but of *when*...

"Rikki?" Sam prodded, apparently not for the first time. "Could you please pass the soy sauce?"

Later that evening, Rikki walked down to the street with Sam to see her off. "I see what you mean," said the lawyer. "She's obsessed with this takeover, isn't she?"

"Yes. And she looks worse than she did two weeks ago, Sam. Those shadows under her eyes... She's not sleeping well." Rikki picked up the Foo to stop her from tying a knot around their ankles with her leash. "She just keeps worrying and thinking about it."

"You can't let her brood so much. If you could get her out for walks, for a little shopping or a lunch out."

Rikki shook her head. "She had the attack while she was shopping, you know. I think she's afraid of something like that happening again, in a crowd or far from a phone."

The elevator opened, and they stepped into the lobby. "If you weren't here to keep her company," Sam observed, "if all she had were the nurses, maybe she'd get bored or lonesome and start venturing out."

"Maybe," Rikki said doubtfully. She followed Sam outside and set the poodle down on the sidewalk.

"And if your father knew your mother was without company, you don't think he'd come home a little earlier?"

"You don't know my father."

"No..." Sam shrugged. "But I do know you, and I know you've got to take care of yourself as well, Rikki. You're looking lower than a..." She glanced down at the poodle. "Than a Foo's knees. You've been down here five weeks now. Why don't you take a break for a week or two and go home? Go see if your neighbor is watering your house plants, sit on the beach."

The cab for which she had phoned turned the far corner and came gliding down the street. Sam caught Rikki's shoulders and pulled her into a brief embrace. "Or even better than that...go see Clay." The taxi stopped beside them. She opened the door, then turned to smile back at her friend.

"I've *told* you..."

Sam shrugged and slid into the cab. "Go do it anyway!" She slammed the door, and the cab pulled away. As she leaned out the window to wave, her grin clearly said *I dare you!*

Rikki frowned after her. *Easy for you to say!*

When Rikki and Foo returned to the apartment, her mother was just ending a phone call in the living room. "I love you, too," she murmured and put the receiver down. With a sigh she leaned back in her chair, her eyes focused on nothing.

"Dad?" Rikki asked from the doorway.

Her mother started violently. "Oh, I didn't know you were— Yes, that was your father."

"Not good news?" Rikki unleashed the poodle, who bounded across the room to her mistress.

"No..." As the Foo turned around twice in her lap, then settled down, she tried to smile. "He'll be back tomorrow,

but he'll be going straight to the office from the airport. I
suppose we'll see him in the evening.''

If we wanted to wait up, Rikki thought wryly. But seeing
the look on her mother's face, she went to her and sat on the
footrest by her knees. "It's okay, Mom. Even if this deal
didn't work out, Dad will find a way. Please don't worry.''

"But he has so little time left . . .''

"He'll find a way," Rikki repeated with a confidence she
didn't feel. She reached out to tug the Foo's ear. "You'll
see.''

"He sent you his love," her mother added. She seemed to
hesitate for an instant, then added in a rush, "And he
wanted to know if by any chance . . . you'd seen Clay again.''

Rikki let go of the poodle's ear and sat upright. She let
out a hiss of exasperation but didn't speak.

"I said you had . . . last night, but that you hadn't mentioned anything that might be a help . . .''

Yes, while Clay had been saving her from a pack of young
thugs, she should have been trying her hand at corporate
espionage! But her mother didn't know that Clay had saved
her last night. Rikki had thought it wiser to gloss over the
affair altogether. "Mom, even if I did know something . . .''

Elizabeth Casey leaned forward so abruptly that the
poodle scrambled off her lap. "He's a *young* man, Rikki!
Clay's got all the time in the world to rebuild, if he loses this
time. And he did start this, after all! To whom do you owe
your loyalty?''

She had never seen her mother burn so fiercely. But, then,
her father had never needed protecting before, had he?
Rikki put up a placating hand. "Mom, I don't know anything that would help Dad. Truly, I don't.''

Her mother searched her face. "But you could find out,
couldn't you? Perhaps if you visited him at his office?''

"I doubt it. Clay's no fool, you know." *Please don't try to push me into this! Please don't.* Rikki held out her hand again. "Now why don't we go to bed? It's been a long day."

For a miserable moment she didn't think that her mother would take her hand. And when at last she did, Rikki found that it was almost too easy to help her out of her chair. She weighed nothing at all, although she was taller than her daughter. She wasn't eating enough, was worrying herself to a shadow. *This has to be stopped!*

Elizabeth Casey persisted. "Just go see him. That's all I ask."

Rikki sighed. "Mom . . ."

"That's all I ask." Her mother turned and walked proudly out of the room, head high, her poodle trotting at her heels.

Rikki stood very still. No, that wasn't all her mother was asking. Wearily, she walked over to the light switch. At the far end of the room she could see herself reflected, tiny and imperfect, in the panes of the French windows. *To whom do you owe your loyalty, Erika Casey?*

"JUST SEE HIM. That's all I ask."

Rikki thought about little else the following day. To see him . . . it was a hunger that nothing else could appease. She picked up the phone more times than she could count, but each time she put it down again. For seeing Clay would not be enough. She needed his smile, his touch, his attention, as well. She needed his love. And for a little while, at least, he would give her that gladly, if she asked.

But then what? To accept his loving would be to weld the final link in the chain that already bound her to him. *I won't love a man like that. I won't!* So each time she put the phone down again. That day lasted roughly three lifetimes.

Night brought her no relief. When she slept at all, it was a light and restless sleep, tormented by dreams. Some time near dawn she found herself hurrying through an airport. It was early morning in her dream as well.

She was forcing her strides, almost running to keep up with a tall man who walked too fast. Far overhead, a loud-speaker blared something unintelligible, threatening. Hurrying footsteps echoed on marble, and a baggage cart came reeling out of the shadows like a wheeled and rumbling monster. *Don't go!* She couldn't say the words. She tried to speak them aloud, but her throat had closed—her lips wouldn't shape them. Then they were outside, standing below a plane, its wings blotting out half the sky. Its silver sides glowed pink as the sun rose. The man stooped to her level to kiss her and as he did so, she saw his face at last. It was Clay. He smiled remotely, rose to his feet, turned and strode across the tarmac toward the stairs of the plane, and she would have run after him, but someone was holding her. Holding her while she soundlessly wailed. *Don't go!*

Or maybe she screamed it aloud this time. For the air was filled with screaming now—the engines of the plane were shrieking, the pitch rising higher and higher. The jet wash blew back her hair as the air shredded around her. Sound sliced at her ears. "Let's go inside," someone said, but she couldn't. She wouldn't. She had to wave.

But which window was Clay's window? All the plane's windows were blank, reflecting the sunrise. She was waving, waving, and all the time she waved, she knew that he couldn't see her, that he sat on the far side of the plane. That he already had his briefcase open on his knees, and he was not looking out the window anyway. Still she waved as the plane backed away from her, shrieking its indifference, its need for the skies and for endless blue distance.

When the jet was only a tiny speck in the sky, Rikki woke with tears on her cheeks.

For a while she simply lay there, her hands clenched in the rumpled bedsheet. Finally she rolled over and sat up. She would go out on the terrace. She needed air, sunlight . . . *Clay* . . .

A few minutes later, dressed in her bathrobe, Rikki carried her coffee outside. It was almost six-thirty by the kitchen clock.

Her father stood at the edge of the terrace, a mug steaming on the stone balustrade beside him. Although he must have come in some time after midnight, he was dressed for the office already.

"Hi, stranger." Coming to stand beside him, she set her coffee beside his. They exchanged smiles, hers still sleepy, his weary, then both of them turned to the street below. At this hour it was deserted except for a gray cat prowling between the closely parked cars. Rikki looked up. The sun had risen already, although, of course, the buildings blocked it. Overhead the sky was softened by clouds and washed a pale, translucent blue. It would grow duller as the day's smog accumulated.

"I'm sorry the deal with Harrison didn't work out," she said.

"Yes, well..." John Casey picked up his mug and drank, then set it down again. "Thanks."

Was he angry with her, thinking her a traitor to his cause, or only too tired to elaborate? She stole a glance at his profile. It was as stern and aloof as always. No more so, nor less, for all the lines of exhaustion that creased it. She sighed and looked at the street again. Below, the gray cat had found a pigeon to stalk. It sank down on its haunches behind a garbage can, its tail twitching. It was so *hard*—almost impossible—to see her father as a pigeon to be stalked and taken by Clay. And if this was hard for her to envision, how much harder, how much more painful, must it be for her father? "Dad... if you lose Strategix, what will you do?"

His shoulders jerked, then he buried his face in his mug again. He put it down with a click that surely chipped the glaze on its base. "I don't know, Rikki. I don't know... But I do know one thing..."

She looked at him silently, waiting.

His voice was harsher than normal, but low, as if his words were only for her to hear. "I know that I won't go out a failure... This may be the end of a chapter, but I'll be *damned* if it's the end of my book!"

That was just what she feared—and what her mother feared. After such a setback, any other man might decide enough was enough and go home to his well-earned retirement, but—oh, no—not John Casey. Not the Hard Case. But if he meant to start over from scratch, it would take him the rest of his life to again reach his present pinnacle of power.

And while he was struggling back to the top, he would be an invisible man, as far as those who loved him were concerned. For her mother's sake, that prospect was too awful to accept. "I suppose there's still a chance that you might win," she said hastily. "I understand that the shareholders are beginning to respond to your tender. The *Journal* said you've been offered thirty five percent of VenturiCo as of yesterday."

"I'll win only if I can stop McCann from buying me first." Below them, the cat had crept to a doorway only a few feet from his prey. The pigeon pecked on in bird-brained oblivion. Her father let out his breath in what could almost have been called a sigh. "You know, it's funny— would be funny—if somehow I pulled it off, buying VenturiCo. I've always told myself I wouldn't retire until I had a year with twenty billion in sales." He glanced at her almost shyly, then looked away again.

Her mouth dropped, but no words came out. Her father, considering retirement?

"The funny thing is, if I did win this takeover, I'd make my goal. The combined earnings of Strategix and VenturiCo would put me well over the top."

"You'd retire if you won this takeover?" she demanded incredulously.

Startled by the intensity in her voice he turned to face her. His eyes sharpened as he seemed to realize this wasn't a hypothetical conversation. "Well, maybe that's too strong a word," he said quickly. "Maybe slow down is more what I meant."

"How do you mean?" she insisted.

He frowned. "I suppose I might give up being chief executive officer, the day to day operations. I could keep my hand in as long as I kept the chairmanship of the board."

"Would that mean you could spend more time at home?"

He looked dubious. "It might be possible to cut back to four office days per week."

She caught his arm. "Is that a promise, Dad? Would you really do that?" Three day weekends, her mother could live with that. Why, that would almost double the time he now spent at home.

He retreated half a step. "No, it wasn't. It was just a thought."

She clung to his sleeve. "You've never wanted something so bad, that you'd offer something important to get it? Where you'd say, if I could *just* have that, I would—"

"No," he said flatly, as he detached his sleeve from her fingers. "No, Rikki, generally I don't try to bargain when I pray."

Oh, if only you would this time!

Seeing the look on her face, he tried to smile. "No, if I want something badly, I try to remember that God helps those who help themselves. So...I guess I'd better get to the office." He kissed her cheek with an awkwardness that reminded them both of how long it had been since he'd last done that. Then he marched briskly from the terrace.

Oh, if only he would! Thoughtfully, Rikki turned back to the view of the street below. The cat sat licking its coat with an air of cool disdain. The pigeon had flown away.

CHAPTER EIGHT

"JUST SEE HIM."

But that wasn't all her parents were asking. She couldn't spy. Not on a friend. Not on Clay.

But she could tell him one last time, this has got to be stopped. He would not listen, but at least she would have done all that she could. Would have seen him. Would have tried...

So... Rikki took a deep breath and stared up at Clay's building, then looked down again hastily as it seemed to sway toward her. So... She had come here without conscious planning, had told herself that she was merely going to South Street Seaport, to have a drink by the river and see the ships. But somehow the proximity of Wall Street, of the building that housed Clay's headquarters, had worked on her like a magnet. After the drink she had decided that she needed a walk, and inevitably her feet had carried her here.

She looked at her watch. He won't be here. It's after six. But she knew better. He was here. It was the man himself, not his building, that had dragged her to this spot. Feeling like a diver on the high board, she took another deep breath, then walked into the lobby.

But it wasn't quite that easy. The top floors of the building were served by a private elevator. Apparently you couldn't just walk in off the street and drop in for a visit. "I won't be on that list," she assured the security guard who asked for her name. She had tried, anyway... Half-relieved, half disappointed, she turned to go, but the man put out a hand.

"Carr, Carter, Casey. Erika Casey—that's you, isn't it?" He looked up from his approved list, obviously pleased that he could admit her.

So Clay had anticipated her visit, she reflected as the elevator whispered skyward. Somehow she found this more disturbing than flattering. Had he known she would come to him?

That feeling of being expected intensified when the elevator door opened on the sixty-first floor. A woman stood waiting for her. Though of course, all that really meant was that the security guard had phoned ahead.

The silver-grays and blacks of the VenturiCo vestibule set off the sleek brunette to perfection. "Miss Casey? I'm Mr. McCann's executive secretary. Would you step this way, please?"

So this was Clay's world. It was altogether different from her father's offices. The Strategix offices had evolved over decades. They now had that lived-in look. The walls were studded with business mementos and trophies, photographs of Strategix's aircraft and division managers. Trade journals and business magazines formed untidy stacks in the reception rooms. VenturiCo headquarters, on the other hand, looked all of one piece, polished—as if it had been bought yesterday off some very expensive shelf. Consciously or unconsciously, its decorator had created a look of machinelike power—heartless and seamless, very hard-edged, ultramasculine. Elegant, but utterly impersonal. If this was Clay's chosen world, then she didn't know him at all. She had been a fool to come here.

"Mr. McCann will be with you in just a moment," the woman assured Rikki. She opened a massive ebony door at the end of the corridor and indicated that she should enter.

Clay's office did little to cheer her. The only sense of the man that she got from it was a magnificent ship model that graced one wall, and his choice of a view. Rikki drifted to the bank of windows. From here Clay could look down on the ships of South Street Seaport and on the East River. Otherwise, the room had no personality. It was as beautiful and impersonal as a suite in a deluxe hotel—Clay had not made himself at home here. She turned her back on the chilly room and stared at the river. She was crazy to come here! She didn't want to see him like this. At least from her father's offices, you could tell that he loved his work. This place felt heartless—it was just a machine for making money. *I didn't want to see him like this. Oh, I want the Clay I knew on the* Princess! Far below, a sailboat came gliding down the river, swept along on the outgoing tide. It looked about the size of craft that Clay had wanted once upon a time in that innocent world of so long ago.

How could he have given up that world of sunshine and adventure for this? The door clicked behind her and she turned.

"So you came." Clay McCann stood with his back to the door he had just entered. Against its ebony panels, his hair gleamed like tarnished bronze, but his eyes were lost in shadow.

"Yes..." The word came out so softly, she wondered if he heard it.

He came away from the door with a little lunge and moved lithely toward her. There was something so purposeful in his movements that she might have retreated, if she hadn't had the window at her back.

"You took your own time about it," he growled, as he caught her arms and pulled her against him.

She was coming home, as his body enfolded hers, and yet she couldn't stay there, shouldn't be there. "I came to—"

"Yes," he agreed, with that undercurrent of laughter she loved so in his voice, and he kissed her.

All the words she'd prepared came apart in her mind, disintegrated into sounds, letters, shreds of meaning that

blew away on the winds of his kiss. With a little moan she
closed her eyes. All that mattered, all that existed was here
between them, here in his breath, which she inhaled, in the
solid warmth of his body, the arms that held her arched up
against him. Here was comfort and joy and belonging. Here
and nowhere else. Yes . . .

Only when he loosened his hold did she open her eyes. His
arms slid down to lock behind her waist, keeping her close
against him. She had to brace her hands on his chest and
lean backward to see his face. "Rikki." Clay spoke her
name not as a prelude to talk. The sound of it seemed
enough in itself to him. His gaze moved over her with a kind
of hungry satisfaction, as if he were possessing her with his
eyes. "You took your time getting here!" His mouth curled
at the corners, then he bent forward to brush his nose across
her cheek as if testing its smoothness. "And you've chosen
a hell of a time to come, I'm afraid. I have a conference in
ten minutes."

Reality sliced through the golden haze of his presence.
Yes, he had a conference. He would have.

"Tell you what . . ." Clay swung her around, so that her
side rather than her back was to the window. He jerked his
chin at the view below. "That's my place down there, the
building just this side of the Fulton Fish market. See it—the
gray one?"

"Yes . . ."

"The penthouse on the river side is mine. Why don't you
take my keys, wait for me there? This meeting will take a
couple of hours, an hour and a half if I push them, and then
I'll be free . . . for the rest of the night." His arms hardened
as he spoke, almost squeezing a gasp from her.

So that's what he thinks! Rikki turned her face aside as he
bent to kiss her again. Finding her mouth unavailable, he
transferred his attention to the side of her neck, tracing its
length with one slow, burning kiss that set her shuddering
all over. "That's not—that's not why I came, Clay!" Her

words came out in a husky echo of her usual speaking voice. Her hands had clenched on the lapels of his charcoal-gray suit, crumpling their crispness.

"No?" Laughter shimmered in his voice again. Plainly he did not believe her.

"No, it isn't." Somehow she found the resolve to shove him back an inch or two. When he moved to kiss her, she flinched.

That caught his attention, and his brows tilted in question. "Oh?" A ledge ran at waist height in front of the windows. Without letting her go, Clay propped his hips against it. He pulled her between his braced legs. "So... what did you come here for?"

She was stingingly, thrillingly aware of his arousal. As if to make her more fully aware of it, he slid his hands down to her hips and pulled her to fit snugly against him. "Hmm?" he inquired matter-of-factly.

She couldn't find words for a moment. Words weren't a part of the language they were speaking as Clay met her gaze frankly. *I am a man, and you are my woman,* those blue eyes told her. *And that is precisely the way it should be!* his warm lazy smile added.

"What did you come for?" he asked again. His eyes dared her to find a coherent answer, looked smugly pleased when she could not.

"I..." She held herself absolutely still against him. "I...came...here to..." The words seemed to dissolve in her mind as fast as she could form them. "To...tell you to stop."

"Stop my tender?" His teasing smile faded. Clay shook his head in the smallest of arcs, his eyes never leaving her face. "You know I can't do that." His hands tightened on her bottom almost cruelly. "You *know* that, don't you?"

"Yes." She'd known it was useless. But now she had tried. What more could she do?

Clay was following a slightly different train of thought. "So if you knew that all along, then that's not why you're here."

There was enough truth in his reasoning to send the blood rushing to her face.

"Mr. McCann?" a female voice called seductively.

"Dammit!" Clay murmured, more to himself than her.

Rikki would have whirled around, but Clay's hands held her effortlessly in place. Whipping a mortified glance over her shoulder, she could see no one.

"Mr. McCann," the voice continued. "Mr. Oglethorpe and his associates have arrived. They are waiting for you in the conference room." The intercom switched off with a tiny click that Rikki caught this time.

For one heartbeat, Clay stood utterly frozen, an odd look on his face. As if he were doing sums in his head, or was searching for some way to stop time. Then his chin jerked in some sort of inner dismissal, and his blue eyes refocused on her. "That's not why you're here, Rikki. We both know that."

"You are the most arrogant man I've ever met!" He was also correct, which only made her humiliation the more complete. She leaned against his hands. "Now if you don't mind—"

His hands slid up to a less intimate hold on her waist. He allowed her to back off half a step but no farther. "Rikki, it's no use. Don't waste our time acting shocked or outraged—you're straighter than that. You know what you want." His eyes swept from her flushed face to the hair he'd tousled himself, then down over her body. "You know what *I* want," he added huskily. "You know where this is heading, where we'll end up."

They were heading for heartbreak, there wasn't a doubt in her mind. For a moment she would almost have welcomed it, as long as Clay was beside her every step of the way. Hardening her mind against this idiocy, she shook her head stubbornly.

"This has been coming for twelve years now," he told her, ignoring her denial. His eyelids had lowered, turning the blue of his eyes to a shadowed, glittering darkness.

"For *twelve*—" Somehow that shocked her dreadfully at this moment. "I thought you were my friend!" So nothing had been as she'd thought, even back then on the *Princess*!

"I am, Rik. That and more." Clay pushed off the ledge. Straightening to his full height, he hooked one arm around her waist to keep her close, then lifted the other to study his watch.

Rage shot through her, dispersing the bewildered hurt. Even at a time like this, he was giving her only half his mind! The other half was obviously in the conference room with— what was that ridiculous name?—Oglethorpe. She tried to spin out of Clay's hold, but he wouldn't let go. "I *am* your friend," he repeated. "But it looks like you need some reminding. Will you wait for me, so we can talk after this conference?"

"No." The time for talking was past. One way or the other, they had passed that point. The only safe thing was to go, and stay gone.

He gave her a little shake. "Dammit, Rik!" Frowning, he glanced around the office. "I suppose if I tied you up here, you'd holler the place down?"

"You suppose right!" He wouldn't dare! At the same time, she remembered the look of his big hands, showing her how to tie her knots aboard the *Princess*. He was almost capable of it.

"Bad for my negotiating skills anyway," he decided regretfully, "—screaming females. All right, then, tomorrow we talk."

"No."

His face had lost all signs of amusement as they locked eyes. "Yes," he said deliberately. "At length. I'll pick you up at eight."

"No. You won't." If she had never seen this stubborn side of him so clearly before, then neither had he seen hers.

"Since you're apparently allergic to my place, we'll go out. Dress for it."

"Clay, would you cut this out! I'm not going anywhere with you."

He moved toward the door, taking her with him. "But right now, I've got to get some papers together for this meeting."

Hissing with exasperation she dug in her heels for a moment. Than as she realized he was escorting her out, meant to let her go, she went with him. "Damn you, Clay! Do you think you can order everyone around?" She turned at bay at his door.

"Not everyone. Just you," he said coolly. He braced his arms on the door to either side of her and gave her a lopsided grin. She put her hand on the door knob, but the door opened inward. She was trapped here till it pleased him to let her go. "So kiss me goodbye," he told her.

"Huh!" she said rudely. Was this what so much success did to you? His ego was beyond all imagination!

"Come on, Rik," he taunted softly. "Where's the old spirit? Stop running, stop hiding. Face up to it. It's time to stand and deliver."

"Good-bye." It was all she could manage. And this was really goodbye! Suddenly her eyes were swimming, and yet she could not have said if it was from rage or from grief.

"Only till tomorrow." The teasing note had vanished from his voice.

"No, for always." One teardrop trembled on her lashes and fell.

He stared down at her flushed face for a long moment, his eyes following the tear's descent. "Then you'd better kiss me, if that's what you think," he said flatly. Moving closer till their bodies were nearly touching, Clay tilted his head so that his forehead rested on hers. "Hmm? For old time's sake? Don't leave this way, darling."

Perhaps it was the endearment, his first ever. At the thought that it would also be the last she'd ever hear from him, her eyes overflowed. Half blinded, she sought his mouth, the closest source of comfort in a bitter world.

Clay stood absolutely motionless, letting her come to him. Giving her only his willing lips, warmly tender, enchantingly obedient to the demands of her kiss. As she rose on her tiptoes to press closer against him, he made one harsh, muffled sound deep in his throat, a sound almost of triumph. With that Rikki opened her eyes. She broke the kiss abruptly and backed off. "Yes," Clay said simply, as if he'd won the telling point in some argument, and a smile curled the corners of his mouth.

How could she walk out this door, leave this unfolding joy behind forever?

"On second thought, better make it eight-thirty," Clay decided as he reached past her to pull the door open an inch or two. "I have to dash up to Boston in the morning, and that will set the whole day back a bit. I'll be playing catch-up for the rest of the afternoon."

Her eyes flared wide. "Are you deaf, dumb and blind—or simply stupid? I just told you goodbye!"

"I heard you." He opened the door the rest of the way and stood aside to let her step out. She stalked past him, then whirled indignantly, still groping for a response, when he added, "Now do your doorman a favor."

"What?" she snapped. She swiped at her cheeks with the back of one hand, wiping the tears away.

"Don't tell him to try and stop me tomorrow night," Clay warned her cheerfully. "He's a nice guy. I'd hate to have to punch him."

"You're impossible!" she stormed. Spinning away, she left him standing in his own doorway. And impossible to forget?

How can you tell someone goodbye, if he won't go away? Rikki pulled the brush through her hair and stared at herself in the mirror of her dressing table. Her reflection stared back at her, clad in a peach satin camisole and tap pants, with no answer to that question. How can you?

She turned to look at the clock. Eight-ten, and still she hadn't decided what to do... Or was it up to her to decide? If Clay really meant to see her, then he was right, no doorman would stop him. She doubted that he'd punch Harry as he'd threatened, but he'd certainly walk right through him. Clay had an air of command that could topple any doorman's stand. Without a conscious decision, Rikki picked up an eyeliner pencil and leaned forward to apply it lightly.

She could always go out before he got here. But that meant that Clay would encounter her mother instead, when he knocked on their door. Just who would get the best of that interview she could not imagine, but she had no intention of finding out. She'd go out with Clay every night this month, before she'd let him disturb her mother. Putting down the pencil, Rikki reached for her mascara.

Of course, she could have appealed to her father for help this morning, but that was no solution, either. The last thing she wanted to see was a face-off between those two! She swept just a hint of blusher across her cheekbones, then closed the case with a snap. No, she would just have to fight this battle herself, if Clay was going to be so pigheaded.

Turning to her closet, she chose a deep burgundy dress, a silk one with lines so understated that it looked almost severe. She meant to look severe tonight. She needed to feel severe. Buttoning it up, she turned to the mirror again. She looked not so much severe as darkly glowing, expectant—a woman awaiting her lover.

A twinge of guilt shot through her. The image in the mirror bit its bottom lip and looked away. No, that was silly. She needn't be ashamed of the way Clay made her feel. She simply would not let those emotions rule her actions. She must not.

Instead, somehow, someway, she was going to make something crystal clear to Mr. Clay McCann tonight—he was wasting his time. She would not date a man who was out to wreck her father. It didn't matter what his motives were. Even if he saw this takeover bid as strictly business, utterly impersonal, it didn't matter. What mattered was the outcome, and the outcome was becoming all too clear. The *Journal* had reported today that fifty-five percent of Strategix shareholders were now willing to sell their stock to Clay. He had the majority he needed to take control; all he had to do was wait for the legal purchase date.

That was why she'd decided to see him tonight, she told herself. The only reason. Tonight she'd tell him to buzz off—once and for all. He'd made his choice, and now she'd made hers.

And yet still a voice deep down inside her cried, *My choice is you! I choose you, and damn the consequences!*

Slipping into a pair of heels to match her dress, Rikki picked up her purse and walked out of the bedroom. It would be better to meet Clay in the lobby. *To meet Clay* . . . the words were like a song in the heart. She found herself almost dancing as she went to find her mother.

In the living room, Elizabeth Casey sat cross-legged on the carpet, her sketchbook in her lap. Sitting in uneasy splendor on a pillow on the couch, the Foo rolled her eyes at Rikki when she stepped into the room.

"Don't disturb her," her mother said without looking around. "I've finally persuaded her to sit still." She added a painstaking line to her sketch, then another.

"Mom, would you be all right if I went out for a little while?" It shouldn't take long to tell Clay what she had to say. She had been an idiot to dress up like this for the occasion, hadn't she?

"Of course I'll be all right." Elizabeth Casey looked around at her, then blinked. "Oh, Rikki, you look lovely!"

That was why she had dressed, of course. To surprise some such reaction out of Clay. A stupid thing to try to do, if she really meant to tell him goodbye. If... *Oh, God, can I?*

The phone rang. "I'll get it!" she cried.

The poodle bounced to its feet and her mother pointed an imperious finger. "Down, Felicity! You sit down, young lady."

"Hello?" Rikki sat in the chair by the phone table.

"Miss Casey?" It was a woman's voice, smooth, vaguely familiar.

"Yes?"

"Miss Erika Casey?" That smooth voice carried an undercurrent of anxiety.

"This is she." Rikki felt the first stirrings of apprehension.

"This is Irene Gibson, Mr. McCann's personal secretary. I'm afraid I have a terribly belated message to give you. I was supposed to call you several hours ago."

"Yes?" Rikki waited in mounting impatience while the secretary explained that Mr. McCann had tried to phone Miss Casey long distance this morning, and then again between conferences in Boston this afternoon, but that each of his attempts had been met with a busy signal.

Gretta! Rikki thought and gritted her teeth. The nurse had a passion for chatting on the phone.

Finally, Miss Gibson continued, her boss had called his office, and instructed her to keep calling Miss Casey's number until she made contact. But somehow the phone number had been written down incorrectly, and Miss Gibson had been calling the wrong number all afternoon. It was only this evening, when the person who lived at that num-

ber had come home from work, that Miss Gibson had dis-
covered her mistake. Then by dialing several permutations
of the original number she'd finally hit upon the correct
one.

"Yes," Rikki said quickly. "And what was the message,
please?"

The message was that some unexpected business had
come up. Mr. McCann had had to fly on from Boston to
Seattle for a series of meetings, and so had asked Miss Gibson to convey his apologies. Mr. McCann would be tied up
until late this evening, New York time, but he would call her
himself tomorrow. And he would be back in town within a
very few days.

"I see..." Rikki said with fragile precision. "Thank you
very much." She hung up, realizing in the instant she set the
phone down that the woman was still talking, but by then it
was too late. And it didn't matter. What did matter? At the
moment she could not think of one thing... *There's an important call on the other line, Rikki*... He'd *known* how
upset she was yesterday, he'd known. He'd said himself that
they needed to talk... But some unexpected business had
come up. Well, she knew all about business and its brutal
priorities...

"Rikki?" Her mother's soft voice was filled with concern.

What an *idiot* she'd been to ever dream! To ever hope...
Her eyes began to fill and she blinked them desperately.

"Oh, baby, what is it?" Her mother put her pad aside and
started to rise.

Rikki rubbed the back of one hand across her eyes and
tried to smile. "I've just—I guess I've been stood up for an
Oglethorpe!" Or someone just like him—someone with a
briefcase, a business suit, and probably a neglected wife at
home. Oh, what was *wrong* with some men?

"An Oglethorpe?" Her mother wrinkled her brow and
stared at her as if she'd gone mad.

"Just a dumb joke, Mom." Rikki wiped her eyes again, sniffed, then tried to laugh through her tears. "Oglethorpe's just some stupid business friend of Clay's—"

Her mother sat on the ottoman at Rikki's feet, then leaned forward to smooth the hair back from her daughter's face. "He stood you up, baby?"

Her tenderness broke down the last of Rikki's resistance. Nodding rapidly, the tears spilling down her face, she stood abruptly. She had to get out of here! "H-he had to fly to Seattle—" She wiped her cheeks again, forced a ridiculous smile that attempted to reassure and failed miserably. "I'm sorry—" She hurried out of the room.

It was some twenty minutes later that Rikki stepped out of her bedroom again. She was dressed now in jeans and an old cotton shirt whose over-washed softness seemed an essential comfort tonight. She carried a small suitcase. She set it by the front door, then walked down the hallway.

Her mother sat in the chair by the phone, stroking the dog in her lap and staring out the open French doors at the darkness.

"Mom?" Rikki sat on one arm of her chair. "I'm leaving town for a few days. Do you think you'll be all right?"

"Of course I will. Gretta will be delighted to have me all to herself." She put a slender hand on her daughter's arm. "But why, darling?"

Because she had to get away. She had to forget all this before it tore her in half! "I . . . guess I need some time alone..." Her mother knew why. Those luminous gray eyes looking at her were filled with pity and understanding. The hand on her arm tightened comfortingly. "It's only about four weeks till school starts again. Maybe I'll go in one day and rearrange the classroom." She'd done that already, before she left town, but it sounded vaguely plausible. Ah, but what was the use in lying? "There's one thing, Mom...what I said . . . about Oglethorpe? I was upset and being stupid.

Could you maybe just... Could we erase that? I don't know if it has anything to do with Dad and this—"

Her mother's hand tightened almost painfully. "I'm afraid it's too late, Rikki," she said quietly. "I'm sorry..."

"Did you—" But of course she had.

"I called John, yes."

Rikki made a little sound and pulled her hand away. But it was no use in blaming her mother. This was her own fault—her own idiotic fault entirely.

I will be torn in half, if I stay here! Rikki stooped to drop a kiss on her mother's head. "Mom, I'm sorry, but I can't—" She pulled a shaking breath. "I'm gone. I'll call you in a day or so." She bolted for the door.

CHAPTER NINE

RIKKI DROVE north to Providence, Rhode Island, in a state of numbness. Later on she could not remember retrieving her car from the garage, driving out of the city, passing the towns along the Connecticut turnpike or the forests of southern Rhode Island. It was only as she followed the long, elevated curve of Highway 195 through the city of Providence, that she roused enough to note her whereabouts or the time. It was half past midnight. With a weary sigh, she took the exit that led to her apartment building near the head of Narragansett Bay.

She slept like the dead until just before dawn, when the dream returned. Again she tagged through an airport at dawn at the heels of a hurrying, preoccupied man. Again he kissed her with businesslike efficiency and turned away. Again she waved and knew that he didn't even see her wave. Once again the plane departed in awful, beautiful indifference, leaving her lonely, alone and unloved. She woke again to find tears on her cheeks.

But if she could not control her sorrow at night, she could fight it during the day. Her life had been full enough before Clay McCann walked back into it. Satisfying enough, peaceful. Somehow, someway, she was going to retrieve the peace of mind she'd had if it killed her. And from the way Rikki set about retrieving it, she might indeed have been trying to work herself to death.

She spent each day in the echoing solitude of her classroom, preparing for the coming school year. Surrounded by

the familiar tools of her trade, microscopes and slides, textbooks and blackboards, seating charts and lesson plans, she
could tell herself that she was Rikki Casey, successful, vital
teacher—someone with knowledge, warmth and humor to
contribute, even if it was only ninth and tenth graders who
needed her contribution.

In the evenings it was not so easy. Though she took her
textbooks and paperwork home with her each day, when the
sun went down she was not a teacher. She was Rikki Casey,
woman, longing for a man who had more important things
to occupy his life—companies to destroy, empires to build.

Worse yet, she was Rikki Casey, bungler and spy, who
had probably betrayed the man she loved to her father.

Worst of all, each night in her dreams she turned into a
frightened child, pleading shamelessly with Clay not to leave
her. She woke each morning at dawn, her unknown airport
fading around her, desolation filling a heart that seemed too
young and frightened for her body.

The only cure was to get up, take her shower too cold,
drink her coffee too hot and too bitter, while she read the
morning paper and waited for the school building to open
at eight. Work would cure her...eventually.

Work would cure this, rather than play. So she made no
effort to contact her friends. Much as she'd missed them
while she was away, she was not ready to face them yet.
When she could smile again, she would see them. But not
yet. Still, when her phone rang on her second night back,
Rikki hurried to answer it. If Sam had tried to reach her in
New York, she would now know she was in town, or perhaps it was her mother or— "Hello?"

"Rikki." It was Clay's voice. No note of question in it, he
spoke her name as a simple affirmation, but with an undercurrent of unmistakable possessiveness. *You are you, and
you are mine.*

Oh, God. She'd thought it was so hard to face living
without him, when he was out of her life. How much harder

it was, when she had him breathing in her ear, saying her name like that!

"What are you doing up there, when I'm down here?" he demanded.

"Getting on with my life." She hung up the phone. Without giving herself time to think she stooped to disconnect its cord from the wall. The energy born of panic gave out in her and she folded abruptly by the phone jack. *What am I doing up here? When he's down there?* The arrogance of the man! He was like a planet, wondering where its moon had wandered off to, assuming that he'd hold sway over her heart and her orbit forever. *"What are you doing up there, when I'm down here?"* Did he think she couldn't live without him?

She crawled into bed soon after that, dreading her dreams, but too spent emotionally to stay awake. But oddly enough, Rikki did not dream at all that night. She woke late to find the sun shining in her window. Blinking drowsily, for a delicious moment she felt like a cat in the sunlight, existing only in a present of soft sheets and golden light. A sense of the future gathered slowly, like bright motes of dust coalescing in the sunshine to form some vague shape of hope and delight. She'd been promised something... Something wonderful was coming her way... She remembered. Clay. Last night. His call. *"What are you doing up there, when I'm down here?"*

Happiness vanished—dust motes collapsing back into separate atoms of swirling dirt, no more. It was time to get up, to fight the regrets, the very thought of him. A cold shower, coffee, a day of work to be done, these were the things that would save her, the things with which she could fill her mind. And her lifetime? Would they be enough to fill that?

She had completed the morning rituals and was loading her car with the books she meant to take to school that day, when the Porsche turned the corner. Rikki shut the hatchback of her car and stared. No one in her apartment building owned a beauty like this. It must be some friend of— The black, teardrop shape stopped beside her, the driver's window rolled down.

"Going someplace?" Clay McCann inquired.

Rikki bumped into her own car as she backed away. Sagging against its fender she drew a shaking breath. Clay. Here, in her world. If she couldn't escape him here, then where could she?

"Now you're supposed to say, 'How did *you* get here?'" he coached her. He was not smiling. His blue eyes held a look of searching alertness as they flicked over her face and body. But a smile lurked somewhere around the corners of his mouth.

"How did you get here?" she asked dazedly.

"The shuttle flight to Green airport," he told her. His look of satisfaction increased slightly.

"Then how did you— Did you rent—" As she struggled to shape sentences, he shook his head, the grin breaking slowly into view. "You didn't just buy a Porsche to drive over here, did you?" But of course he had.

"The rental cars were boring," he admitted. "And there was a dealership just down the street from the airport . . ."

"How nice for you." Spinning away from him she yanked open her own car's door and slid inside. But she could not pull out from her parking place with the Porsche blocking her way. She clenched her hands on the steering wheel and stared straight ahead. What now? How could she—

"Hey." Clay dropped his hands onto the frame of her open window and leaned down to peer into her face. "What's the matter?"

She shook her head wearily. "Tell me what isn't. Why can't you get it into your head that this isn't going to work— you and me? Why can't you just leave me alone?" Her head drooped forward, until she rested her forehead against the steering wheel between her clenched hands. She was so tired of all this.

Her car door opened. "Hey." Clay's hand found the nape of her neck, stayed there even when she flinched. "Rik, don't take it this way." His fingers explored the rigid muscles of her neck, then started a soothing massage.

"Sure, I'm supposed to just sit back and smile while you destroy my father..." she mumbled and turned her head away from him. That felt so good, his touching her. Did he need to touch her as much as she needed to be touched by him? She bit back a sigh that seemed to well up from her toes.

"Whatever happens, Rik, I'm not going to destroy your father." The car settled as he sat down on the edge of the chassis beside her. The pressure of his fingers increased, authoritative and gentle all at once.

How could she believe that? If he won, then he would destroy her father in the process of winning—it was as simple as that. Even if, by some miracle, Clay lost this battle, it solved nothing.

Her sigh this time was one of pure misery—there was no way this could work out. No doubt Clay loved his company as much as her father loved Strategix. Clay would never forgive her, if her slip of the tongue made him lose it. And at some point she would have to tell him what she had done. She couldn't live with herself otherwise.

Clay's fingers worked down her spine to her taut shoulders. "Is that why you hung up on me last night? You're still worrying about this takeover?"

Her shoulders jerked with a bitter laugh. "You seem to be the only one I know who isn't worrying, Clay! My mother, my father, me... we're all sick with worrying about this. Damn you... why did you have to pick on us?"

He didn't bother to answer that. "Takeover wars don't last forever, Rik. Five more days and this one will be over."

"Four," she corrected him automatically. But the hurt and the damage would last for years after that. Couldn't he see that?

"Is that all that's standing between you and me, Rik? This tender?"

She closed her eyes and inhaled. Did he want that, too, then? Did he want not just her, but want an us? Even if he did, it wouldn't work. Her eyes filled with tears. "No, that's not all. I'm looking for a lover for life, Clay. And I want some companionship out of the relationship. I don't want someone like my father. Like you..." She turned to look at him.

He was sitting very still. His fingers had stopped moving against her shoulders. "How do you mean, like your father?" he asked after a moment. His voice had gone husky, but whether from strain or from sexual tension, she couldn't tell.

"Someone who never has time for me. Who is always at his office, or jetting off to Seattle or wherever on business, just when I need him the most. I won't have it—I couldn't bear it!"

He let out a breath, and his fingers moved against her skin again. "Did you need me the other night, Rik? Is that what you're saying?"

Was it? She couldn't remember. Couldn't remember a time when she hadn't needed this man. She shrugged against his fingers. "Doesn't matter anymore."

His head came up sharply at that, and his lips parted, as if to dispute this. Then, evidently thinking better of it, he closed them again. His eyes moved over her face. "You look awful."

She tried to smile. "Thanks."

Slowly, sensuously, his hand slid up into her hair. His fingers rotated in tiny, rustling circles against her scalp. "You know what you need?"

"What?" she asked unsteadily. She needed him to go on touching her, being tender like this forever.

"You need a day off. And so do I. I'm so tired of fighting with you, Rik. Of arguing. Of even wanting you." His fingers tightened in her hair for an instant, then loosened again. "Do you remember that day in Bermuda, when we just took off?"

Remember it? It had been the best day of her life! She'd never forget it. She nodded slowly against the steering wheel.

"Well, we both need a day like that. We need to run away together. Let's pretend that you're fourteen, and I'm twenty. What do you say?"

"We can't." And yet she wanted a day like that more than anything in the world. More than life itself.

"Sure we can." Clay sounded absolutely certain, utterly sure of himself. He sounded like that same Clay who had taken her hand and pulled her out of the misery of her parents' fight on the *Princess* twelve years ago. The Clay who had turned sadness into joy. He stood and held out his hand. "The secret is that you don't think about it. You just do it. C'mon, Rik."

That day so long ago, she'd thought that she'd follow a man who could do that—turn sadness to joy—anywhere. With that recollection, with no conscious decision, Rikki found her hand unclasping the wheel, reaching for his. And as their hands touched, she could feel the heat jump between them—an electric spark of excitement and hope.

"Now run upstairs," Clay commanded. "Get a towel, a bathing suit and a sweater, and come straight down again. Don't stop to think, don't stop to worry, just come." He glanced at his watch. "I'll give you four minutes—not a second more. Now scoot!"

Don't think, don't think, don't think! He was right to warn her. If she stopped to think, she'd never go with him. Battening her mind against a thousand objections, Rikki threw the clothes he'd suggested into a carryall and grabbed some sunblock. Feeling as if a thousand terrors snapped at her heels and that she could outfly every one of them, she ran back down the stairs.

Clay had the Porsche started already and the door open for her. She slid in beside him and slammed it. "Good girl," he approved. Catching her chin, he dropped a kiss on her lips. Then he slipped the car into gear and they were off.

"I thought we were going to be kids today," she said, keeping her tone as light as his kiss had been.

Clay gave her a sideways grin. "That was entirely in character. Can't tell you how much I wanted to do that, back on the *Princess*!" The Porsche accelerated.

As if by instinct, they headed for the sea. Swooping down the highways, hopscotching over the great bridges, they did not speak much. They had no need for words. But as the Porsche gobbled up the miles, within Rikki the conviction grew—they were not fleeing sadness so much as racing to meet delight. She turned to study Clay's faintly smiling profile. He was magical. How could he do this—turn her world around simply by strolling into it? Simply by being? His was an almost terrifying power, because if he could confer such happiness, then he could also take it away. *Stop!* she warned herself. *Don't think.* Later she would worry, but not today. Today was for feeling, not for thinking. Today was for looking and being and sharing. Clay was right, she had needed a day like today. They topped the high bridge over the Sakonnet River and the view opened out below them, the bay as blue as heaven, glittering like the gates to paradise.

In Newport, Clay parked his car in a parking lot on one of the wharves. They bought cookies and milk at a cookie shop, then ate them sitting on a bench overlooking the harbor.

This was happiness. Salt air, sunshine, warm oatmeal cookies, a heart-catching view, and someone you loved to share it with. Rikki shied away from that last thought. *Don't think,* she reminded herself. *Just be. Don't think at all.* "This is the best cookie," she murmured contentedly.

"Huh!" Clay's arm dropped around her shoulders with an almost big-brotherly casualness. "If you haven't tried the chocolate chip ones, then you haven't lived yet." He waggled his half-eaten cookie under her nose.

She made the mistake of meeting his eyes as she took the bite. The look in those ocean eyes was not big brotherly at all. Rikki sat back against his arm abruptly. *Don't think. Don't think at all, because if you think about loving him, then you have to think of all the reasons it won't— Now, stop it!*

"The problem with this," Clay murmured at her ear, "is that I don't want to be here. I want to be out there." He nodded at the boats bobbing at their moorings in the outer harbor.

"That would be heaven."

"So let's see what we can do about it." Ignoring a sign that warned off trespassers, Clay led her out one of the piers that jutted into the harbor. Well, it was Clay's show. Rikki felt fourteen again, tagging behind an invincible twenty-year-old. If Clay thought trespassing was all right, then it must be—he was in charge here. Feasting her eyes on the lines of the boats alongside, on their shining brass and lustrous varnish, Rikki stayed close at his heels.

"She's a beauty." Clay stopped to lean on the railing and gaze down at a sailboat tied to the dock below.

"A darling," Rikki agreed, then realized that Clay was addressing the man lounging in her cockpit.

"Looks like a real sweet passage maker," Clay continued, as he studied the boat and its gear. He tilted his head back to inspect her mast, then looked at her owner again.

"She is," the man agreed. Getting to his feet he sauntered forward to stand on the bow and squint up at them. "I took her down to the Caribbean last fall. Just came back a few weeks ago. She did the Bermuda leg in four days.''

Clay whistled a long, slow appreciation. "Do you ever charter her?"

"Once in a while." Her owner ran one hand down the forestay, paused to examine a section of the wire, then glanced up again. "But only to people I know."

Clay grinned. "Would you take a hostage instead? I've got this Porsche out in the parking lot . . ."

"I still can't believe you did that!" Rikki marvelled a half hour later as they powered out of the harbor on *Serendipity*. They had left the sailboat's bemused owner standing on the dock, clutching the Porsche's keys. Rikki had also seen a few substantial bills change hands, but she was sure it was the inducement of an afternoon with Clay's sports car that had won the man over.

"It helps to have money to smooth over the rough spots," Clay agreed peaceably. He turned the wheel slightly, to let a power boat pass them port to port.

Yes, money helped. Was that what had turned him from a fun-loving young man into a corporate raider? Lust for the mesmerizing power that so much money gave him over most people? But she wasn't to think today, she reminded herself quickly. *Just be. Just enjoy.* She inhaled a deep breath to savor the salty air. Standing up in the cockpit, Rikki did a slow rotation, taking in the town stair-stepping up its green hill to the crowning white steeple of Trinity church, taking in the boats dancing at their moorings, or swooping around them like great white butterflies. Gulls soared overhead, two giggling children rowed a dinghy ballasted by an enormous, shaggy dog, the rainbow sail of a sailboarder dodged between the boats. Why couldn't life be like this, simple, carefree and beautiful?

"Remember how to steer?" Clay moved out from behind the boat's wheel and patted the cushion.

She took the helm with Clay sitting close beside her. Once he was sure she was comfortable with it, he went forward to hoist the sails, then hurried back to the cockpit to trim them. "Okay, head off that way," he directed her as he winched in the mains'l. A moment later, he cut the engine. The boat glided on in the sudden silence, a butterfly set free, sun-gilded water chuckling along her sides then smoothing out behind them in a silken wake.

As they rounded the old stone fort at the entrance to the harbor, Clay took the wheel. He set course for the mouth of the bay and the open sea beyond. With the wind blowing his tawny hair back from his forehead, his blue eyes alert to every demand of his craft, he looked not a day over twenty. He looked happy and complete in a way Rikki had not seen for twelve years. Their eyes met. *This is it. This is all. This is what some people seek all their lives and never find.* Clay's eyes flicked back to their course, swept the horizon and his boat in a seaman's swift once-over, then he leaned across to take a kiss from her. A quick kiss. A sailor's kiss stolen from the attention he owed his boat. Rikki's heart spiraled skyward to wheel with the white birds in a world of blue.

"How about lunch?" Clay suggested.

"Right!" Rikki danced down the companionway ladder to get the sandwiches and bottles of ale she'd bought at a deli on the wharf, while Clay had been completing negotiations.

After lunch, Clay put Rikki on the wheel again. *Serendipity* quivered under her hands, responsive to the slightest turn of the wheel, power and grace at her command. She was a dream machine singing a siren's song. *Take me anywhere! Let's run away—run far, far away!*

Standing at the wheel, her legs braced to the heel of the boat and her hair lifting in the wind, Rikki listened to that song while Clay went below to calculate their course on the chart. He came back on deck, took another survey of wind, water and sky. "When we round this buoy, we'll fall off, Rik. Head toward Sakonnet Point."

"Anything you say, captain." Anything at all. She would do anything for a man who could turn sorrow to joy like this. He was a magician, a wizard. A takeover wizard, a small part of her brain reminded her. She slammed the door on it instantly. Today he'd taken her over, and she had never been happier. She altered course as they swept past the last buoy on the eastern side of the channel. Clay eased the sheets, and *Serendipity* settled into a bounding, fluid stride. *If you thought I was moving before, watch this!* the boat seemed to be saying.

They spoke very little that afternoon. Words didn't seem to be necessary between them, were perhaps even a danger. But Rikki had never felt closer to anyone in her life before. They could say all that was needed with just a look or a smile. But as the golden hours passed, like bubbles shimmering then dissolving, in *Serendipity*'s wake, closeness of spirit seemed to call for a closeness of bodies. Clay steered with one hand and held Rikki's hand with the other. His eyes on their course, he seemed not even aware of their handclasp. But his fingers traced and retraced the shape of hers in a subtle, teasing pattern that seemed to melt her very bones.

Closeness of spirit called their bodies closer. Without knowing how or when it happened, Rikki found herself tucked into the crook of Clay's arm, her head thrown back against his shoulder to watch the clouds overhead. The boat swooped over the long, lazy swells—a dream machine. This was all a lovely dream, too beautiful to be real....

Cradled in Clay's arm, rocked by the wind and waves, she must have slept. She was dimly conscious of a long and lovely time passing, then she felt the soft warmth of Clay's lips on her temple. She woke with a smile, stretched and sat up.

A tall green island filled half her horizon.

"Clay!" She turned to stare at him. He smiled, but they had grown too close now for that smile to deceive her. He was nervous.

"Where are we?" She swung around. Blue in the late slanting sunlight, the mainland was just a smudge to the north.

"That's Cuttyhunk." Clay nodded at the island.

"Cuttyhunk!" That was an island off Massachusetts. She had never been there before. They were rounding its rocky shore, entering an open roadstead. She could make out a long channel ahead and the masts of anchored sailboats beyond a low spit of sand. "How far are we from Newport?" She looked down at her watch. It was past six. If it had taken them this long to get here, then to get back to Newport would—

"Ohh, twenty, twenty-five miles?" he hazarded. His voice was too casual.

"Clay..." she said dangerously. What an idiot she'd been to trust him.

He gave her his dazzling grin. "You've never wanted to run away? Really run away?"

"Clay, the man will be thinking we stole his boat! He'll have the Coast Guard out after us."

Clay looked like a boy with his hand caught in the cookie jar. "No, he won't. I told him we might want to keep her for a few days. It's all arranged."

The rhythmic thump she was feeling was not part of the boat's motion, Rikki realized suddenly—it was her own heartbeat. A few days with Clay, no one else in the world, just the two of them together within the confines of this boat. "But—but you can't do that! It's only four days until the takeover! You can't just walk away from your business at a time like this."

"Why can't I?"

Why couldn't he? The words rang with unnatural force and clarity in her mind. He was the boss, after all. No one

told him what to do. Why couldn't he make time for her—
for the two of them—if he chose to? It was a question that
had always hurt and frustrated her as a child, whenever she
had asked for and been denied her father's attention. "You
could?" she asked incredulously. "I mean—you can?"

His grin seemed the answer to all her desires. "Here I
am," he said simply. "Here you are. Who's going to stop
us?"

He *was* magical! Time was the greatest gift of all, and
Clay was giving it to her. To her alone. She felt as if her
heart were expanding inside her, as a sail fills with a great
wind.

"We've got to get the sails down." Clay touched the tip
of her nose. "Wake up and take the wheel, dreamer."

Still too dazzled to speak, she did so. She headed the boat
into the wind as he directed, then held her there with the
engine barely ticking over while he dropped and stowed the
sails.

At last he returned, sat beside her and took the wheel. He
turned the boat slightly, lining them up with the channel's
entrance, then glanced down at her. "We'll pick up a
mooring, instead of going into the docks."

Moored out in the anchorage, *Serendipity* would be their
own island. Out there, they would be as alone as two cast-
aways in paradise. Her stomach was filled with spiraling
butterflies. Her hands were freezing cold. One night with
him and he would own her.

They were entering the long channel now. Cuttyhunk rose
above them, a vision reminding her, with its green height, of
a South Sea island rather than a chunk of New England
rock. Clay squinted ahead, studying the inner harbor.
Throttling back on the engine, he steered slightly to star-
board to let an outgoing sailboat squeeze past.

Her hands were freezing. Rikki drew a shaking breath.
She tried another, struggling to calm herself. They were
passing an abandoned Coast Guard station on the left, and

then—she straightened alertly—a ferry dock. "What time does the ferry leave?" she asked quickly, then waited tautly for his reply. If she stayed aboard with him tonight, he would own her forever.

"Tomorrow morning, sometime," Clay said easily.

She gasped, then recognized the emotion sweeping hotly through her for what it was—relief. Relief, delight, and something close to sheer terror.

Clay turned the boat into the tiny harbor, then met her widened eyes for an instant. His own softened, and he reached out to stroke the tip of her nose. They had no need for words.

CHAPTER TEN

CUTTYHUNK'S landlocked harbor nestled under the twin hills of the island, as if the land had flung out a curving, sandy arm to hug the ocean to its breast. They picked up a mooring on the side farthest from the tiny settlement, and closest to a wild and marshy shore.

"Let's go ashore," Clay suggested once they had given the sails a harbor furl and coiled the lines in the cockpit.

Startled, she turned to look at him. Was this an innocent suggestion—could Clay really want to show her the island at a time like this?

Or perhaps he was as nervous as she was, Rikki speculated while they unshipped the dinghy and he helped her into it. And this was his way of buying time.

But as he rowed them toward the town docks, Clay looked far from nervous. His eyes caressed her legs, moved like a warm and languid hand across her breasts, smiled at their response, then rose to meet and hold her gaze. Blushing under his silent admiration, she turned to look blindly at a boat they were passing, then turned back—she could not stop herself—to watch him row.

He moved with a smooth and surging grace that took her breath away. He was power and control and a barely contained exultation, and now she knew why he was taking her ashore. He was intentionally prolonging the tension and the anticipation they both were feeling. He meant to spin out their magical, stolen day like a golden thread, stretch it taut until it quivered with tension, stroke and pluck it to make it sing, then pull it even tighter.

Clay dug in one oar and the dinghy pivoted smoothly, coming to its bobbing rest beside a floating dock. He shipped the oars, then leaning forward, touched Rikki's knee with one cool fingertip.

A line of fire shot up the inside of her thigh as she sucked in her breath. She wanted—no, she needed—him to put his whole hand on her, to cup her kneecap in his big, warm palm. Instead, he traced a teasing, searing path to the underside of her knee and tickled her there.

She swallowed a small sound of protest as his hand feathered away. "Want to go back to the boat?" he challenged softly.

If she admitted it, would she be the loser in this game he was playing? She didn't dare to need him more than he needed her. "Not yet," she said, but the words betrayed her. Her voice was hesitant, far too husky.

His eyes crinkled. "Then up the ladder with you!" He jerked his chin at the ladder that led to the pier above.

If her legs would still hold her! Her knees were shaking, her insides quivering, as if a whole ocean rocked and surged restlessly within.

On shore there was no one in view except a man stacking lobster pots on the wharf where they had landed the dinghy. While Clay chatted with the fisherman, Rikki studied the winding one-lane road that led steeply uphill. All she could see above her were cottages, tucked among the island's greenery. Their shingles were weathered a lovely silver gray by the endless salt winds, or were painted in sun-bleached pastels. The silence enclosing her was rich and tangible, composed of a medley of gentle sounds when she stopped to listen—a whisper of sea breeze, the shimmering cry of crickets, a dog barking in the distance...the soft, deep sound of Clay's question and the fisherman's response.

"Rikki, come over here," Clay called. Out on the wharf he stood in front of a small blackboard fixed to the wall of a shed. He nodded at the fish listed for sale. "What shall we eat tonight, lobster or swordfish?"

The boy who ran the tiny fish market watched them with friendly interest while Rikki considered. With swordfish she would have to devise a recipe. Lobsters, you simply boiled. "Lobsters," she suggested.

"Nice and simple," Clay approved. He turned back to the boy. "Two lobsters, please. The pound and a halfers."

While Clay went back to the dinghy to stow the bag of lobsters, Rikki chose a road at random. Supper would be swift and simple, and after that? She felt her body warming all over, then a hand caught her own.

"Good," Clay said. "This is the way I wanted to go."

He led her silently up the hill. The sun had dropped beyond the hilltop. Blue light pooled to lavender shadows under the eaves of the houses and on their tiny, gingerbread-trimmed porches. Most of the island people seemed to be inside at supper. The smells of cooking mixed with the scents of honeysuckle and of drying kelp. From an open window, the sound of a tenor saxophone floated out into the twilight, achingly tender, wistful and sexy. Clay chose a path that branched away from the cottages. They followed a stone wall that climbed skyward through cricket-loud fields. Ahead, one flaming cloud crowned the hilltop.

"Just in time," Clay said as they reached the crest.

"Oh . . ." He had brought her to the top of the world—a world of radiant water stretched away on all sides below them. Islands and the distant mainland were dark, velvety shapes floating on a sea of quicksilver and amethyst. As they turned to take it all in, the sinking sun bathed their faces in a honeyed glow. He had brought her here to share solitude and beauty, and she could imagine no greater gift. "Oh, Clay . . . it's . . ."

There was a boulder at the very top of the hill. Clay sat on it and pulled her to sit between his legs. Wrapping his arms around her, he rested his chin on her head. "Yes," he agreed, laughter shimmering in his voice. "I thought you'd like it."

"*Like* it!" She turned within the circle of his arms to scan the horizon, then shivered with the beauty of it all. Clay kissed the nape of her neck. She shivered again, and his arms tightened warmly around her. If she could just stay like this, be with him like this for always. If they could just run away forever....

A movement downhill caught her eye. A dark, graceful shape stepped out of the bushes and lifted its nose to catch their scent. "Clay?"

"I see it," he murmured in her ear. "The island's full of deer. See the little one behind her?"

They stayed transfixed on their hilltop until doe and fawn faded back into the bushes. Then they lingered to watch Venus open one silver eye in the west. Finally, with darkness gathering around them, they sighed and got to their feet. Clay chose a different route to the harbor, an unpaved, narrow lane that curved around the island's shoulder, avoiding the town. They walked with their arms wrapped around each other's waists, their steps in soft agreement. Cricket sound filled the balmy air. Halfway back, they came upon three deer grazing along the edge of the track. The animals lifted their heads, snorted, then bounded away from them down the road.

They followed quietly. This time, when they came near the creatures, the deer did not run. They simply turned and walked on. Leading the way silently over the hill, the black, enchanted silhouettes turned every so often, as if to make sure that the humans still followed. In the darkness Rikki felt as if they all might make a wrong turn and follow the deer into the star-sprinkled pastures of the sky. But when the road curved back to the harbor, the deer melted into the shadows and were gone.

The spell of enchantment held as Clay rowed them out to *Serendipity*. The harbor was alive with phosphorescent plankton, and each dip of the dinghy's oars churned tiny galaxies into motion. They spoke not a word, but Rikki found her tension rising with each stroke of the oars through the starry water. At the boat Clay climbed out of the dinghy first, then leaned over to give her his hand. She came up lightly, face to face with him in the darkness, her breath suddenly coming faster as she stared up at his shadowed eyes. His hand caressed down the length of her bare arm, then lightly up again. "Cold?" he asked softly.

"Yes."

He did not take her in his arms to warm her as she'd expected. As she had hoped. Instead, he went below for her sweater and handed it up the companionway to her, along with a large pot. "Would you fill this with seawater, Rik?"

When she had done so, Clay set it to heat on the stove in the galley. Then he busied himself with lighting a brass anchor light and suspending it over the cockpit on a topping lift. Lit by the lantern's warm glow he looked at her from the top of the cabin where he stood. "All right?" he asked quietly.

No, I'm so frightened! I need you to come to me. Hold me. Love me. Make me believe we could be this way forever.... But she couldn't tell him—was afraid to speak at all for fear her voice would give her away. She nodded silently.

"Can you make us a vinaigrette? The owner seems to have the basics aboard. We could toss that with a can of green beans I found, and then there's bread and butter. And he said we could help ourselves to the wine cellar he keeps in the bilge."

"Of course." She slipped below. It was warmer in the galley, and she threw her sweater aside. While she found olive oil, vinegar and mustard in the shelves behind the

stove, Clay uncorked a bottle of chardonnay. He handed her
a filled wineglass, then collected his own.

Lightly, he touched his to hers, and the thin cry of crystal tingled throughout the cabin—seemed to tingle in her
blood, starting a vibration there. "To..." His voice trailed
away as he looked down at her.

Was he as scared as she was? she wondered suddenly. She
didn't know if that thought heartened her or frightened her
more. "To smooth seas," she murmured, a safe toast for
sailors.

"And to us on them." Their eyes held over the rims of the
glasses as they drank.

He was definitely nervous, and suddenly she was glad.
The seawater was simmering in the pan. It was time to boil
the lobsters, but her stomach fluttered with butterflies—
food was the last thing on her mind. If he was nervous, then
this truly mattered to him....

Rikki reached to put the vinegar away behind the stove
and grazed her forearm against the pot. She flinched.
"Oooh!"

"Damn, Rikki! Are you all right?" He caught her arm.

"Yes, just a burn..."

"Let's get some cold water on it." Swiftly, Clay wet a
cloth at the galley pump and laid it over the burn. "Here—
sit." He pushed her down on the settee that flanked one side
of the boat and knelt before her, still holding the cloth in
place. "Let me see it."

By the light of the kerosene lantern that lit the cabin, the
burn was a red, quarter-shaped blotch, no more. "It's
nothing, Clay," she assured him as he frowned at it.

"You're sure?" Lifting her arm to his lips, he kissed her
wrist, just above where it hurt.

Her body began to burn in a different way. "Yes, I'm
sure," she whispered.

"Good. If anything happened to you, Rik..." Warm and
slow, his lips moved against her pulse point. Then, when her

breathing quickened, they wandered up her wrist to her hand. She cupped his living breath in her palm, trembled, then trembled again as his tongue drew a line of liquid fire across her skin.

"Clay..." Melting swirls changed to the erotic pressure of teeth, as he nibbled his way slowly along her fingers to her fingertips. She put her other hand to his face and framed his lean jaw with her fingers, her body trembling all over as the roughness tickled her skin. He caught her wrist and brought that hand to his mouth for a kiss, then he buried his face against her palms. He breathed out a groan of such relief and satisfaction against her that she found herself laughing in wordless joy.

"Yes," Clay agreed, his voice shimmering with laughter, too. "It's been like that, waiting for you." His head came up. Moving slowly, as if a sudden move might frighten her, he rested his hands on her bare kneecaps. She sat very still, looking down at him.

He'd been waiting for her? She'd been waiting for him all her life. *Clay!*

Slowly he rose to his knees before her. Slowly, so slowly and surely, his hands smoothed up the outsides of her thighs, skimmed over her shorts, then curved to cup her hips. "Come closer, darling." He drew her out to the edge of the settee to meet him. "Yes, like that." With his elbows, he pressed her legs in, till they clasped the hard warmth of his waist.

Oh, yes! She touched his face with her hands and bent to meet his kiss. *Oh, yes, my darling!* Her hands twined into his hair, holding him close. She kissed his eyes, his forehead, his mouth, lingeringly, longingly. Oh, Clay! Could it really be? She laughed and arched her neck as his lips moved to her throat, sending a liquid, shuddering convulsion across her body. Yes, it could be. Tonight she could believe it. This was so much more than desire, this was a need so much deeper and stronger and surer than anything she had ever known.

His lips trailed down the collar of her shirt, to where the button blocked his way. With shaking fingers, she unfastened that button for him, then the next. Tonight there was nothing she would withhold from him. All that was hers was his . . . her heart, her soul, her body, her dreams . . . Yes.

"You're so beautiful!" He slipped her shirt down off her shoulders and let it fall. "*So* beautiful . . ." He unclasped the catch between her breasts with fingers that shook ever so slightly, then removed her brassiere in one gliding caress of her bare arms and shoulders. In the lamplight, his eyes seemed to darken. Slowly, almost reverently, he reached out to run one fingertip across the slopes of her breasts. "Rikki . . ." With a sudden movement, he stood, then stooped to pick her up.

Limp as a stroked cat, with eyes half-closed, she arched her neck over the arm that supported her, silently inviting his kiss. Clay drew in his breath on a hiss, his face drawn as if in anger. His eyes moved over her in one fierce, possessive sweep, then he bent to meet her. "*Mine* . . ." he growled against her lips. "No turning back now, darling."

No, there was no turning back, even if she'd wanted to. He invaded her, claimed her, took all that she offered, then demanded more. Behind her closed eyelids, the world had seemed all ruddy gold. Now it darkened to a swirl of red-black that expanded in dark, concentric circles. She breathed only at his pleasure, sucking in great gulps of air that seemed golden and fiery . . . then he dragged her under again. *Yours* . . .

When at last he tore his mouth away, she whimpered in protest, but he was moving on. His lips were on her throat, tasting and testing its softness, lingering to explore each time she gasped and curled closer against him, her fingers digging into his shoulder. When he reached the soft hollow where her pulse hammered, he paused, caressing her, taunting her with his tongue as if he could goad her blood to even wilder revolutions.

The world was whirling faster and faster, roaring, and Clay was the center of that mad race. His lips crept downward, so slowly she cried aloud. Hot, slow, as irresistible and as merciless as lava, his lips inched down the slope of her breast, and he laughed deep in his throat when she squirmed and lifted her breasts, begging for release. If anything, his lips slowed more, swirling over her in teasing digressions while she trembled and twisted in his arms. The blood was roaring in her ears—she hated him, loved him... His lips closed around her at last... His groan almost drowned out her wavering cry of exultation.

No, there was no turning back now. She was his forever. Arms clasped tightly around his neck, she strained up against him, offering herself, begging him to take her—take her now. The blood was thundering in her ears, the world spinning red and golden as he turned to carry her to the wide vee berth in the forward cabin.

The roaring grew louder. Clay stopped and looked toward the open companionway. "Damn!" he said softly. Without putting her down, he moved over to the lamp and blew it out. Then he moved to the stove and switched off its flame and stood there rigidly in the darkness.

"What is it?" she whispered. But what it was was all too clear now—she could hear a dinghy with an outboard motor coming alongside.

"Visitors." Clay set her down on the settee and sighed. "Don't go away, darling." He climbed halfway up the ladder to thrust head and shoulders out the open companionway.

Don't go away—right! Rikki huddled against the cushions, suddenly cold without his arms. She groped for her shirt but couldn't find it in the dark.

"Ahoy, *Serendipity!*"

"Yes?" Clay could not have sounded less welcoming.

"You're Mr. McCann?" a boy's voice demanded.

"I am. What's up?"

"I gotta message for you. A lady rang up the marina. Says you got to call her. Says her name is Gibson, and its an emergency."

Gibson—Irene Gibson, his secretary! Down below, Rikki crossed her arms tightly across her chest. But how could Clay's secretary have found them out here? This cruise had been an impulse—a lovely, serendipitous whim, nothing Irene Gibson could have known about. On deck, she could hear Clay cursing with an absolutely astounding fluency.

"Well, gee, don't blame me, mister!" the boy objected.

"I know, I know, I'm not. Just let me get my wallet." Clay stamped down the companionway ladder. "You heard?" he growled. He seemed to be groping for something—his wallet, no doubt—on the shelf by the chart table.

"I heard..." She couldn't keep the chill out of her voice. The chill was everywhere, spreading throughout her limbs, freezing her heart, her mind, her foolish hopes. An emergency, the boy had said. A business emergency, of course. Something *important* must have come up. She hugged herself so hard that it hurt. "How did she know how to find you?"

He found what he was looking for and crossed to stand in front of her, a big, black shape in the darkness. "I told her we'd be sailing to Cuttyhunk. Called her while you were buying our sandwiches."

He had called her! Rikki's heart was a block of ice. The breath had frozen in her lungs. Clay had called Irene Gibson. That meant he'd planned from the start to be available to his business, should something *important* come up. She sucked in a shuddering breath, exhaled it again and was amazed that it didn't cloud the cabin air. She felt so cold inside. Something important. So *she* was what he did when nothing important was on the agenda. He hadn't really given her his time—it had merely been on loan until it was needed for something that mattered. She had been such a fool.

Clay touched the top of her head, drew his hand down to her cheek. "I'll be back as quick as I can, Rikki. I'm sorry."

Not half as sorry as she was! She had been such a fool.

"Forgive me?" He rubbed her bare shoulder, but she ducked away from his touch.

Someplace beneath the sheet of ice that covered her soul, a red lake of anger simmered—anger more for her own foolish self then for him. But she had no way to express it—the words jammed in her throat like shards of shattered ice. She shook her head, not caring if he could see the motion in the darkness.

"No?" Softly, Clay's hand smoothed down to her breast. Before she could think to draw back, his hand cupped around her in a gesture that was as possessive as it was tender. "Guess I'll just have to earn my forgiveness the hard way, then." There was the ghost of a laugh in his voice. She drew in her breath sharply, preparing to blast him, but his fingers trailed away with a parting caress that seemed to echo throughout her body. "Be back as quick as I can, love." She heard him spring lightly up the ladder to the cockpit. A moment later, the dinghy roared away.

She found her shirt and dressed with shaking hands. She had been such a fool. To dream that she could have all his attention and love—it had been a crazy dream. He wasn't that kind of man, and she had recognized that almost from the start. Tonight she'd been closing her eyes, entertaining a willful, idiotic blindness to what he really was.

The air was not cold, she knew that, but still it held a dampness that seemed to bite to the bone. Rikki pulled a blanket off the vee berth and dragged it to the main cabin, where she huddled beneath it. She would sleep here tonight. The settees were too short for Clay's length, so he could have the vee berth. Forgiveness—he thought he'd earn forgiveness? He'd been ready to take all of her, everything she was and ever hoped to be, while he . . . he had only been on loan. She pulled the blanket tighter around her, but it didn't help.

In the darkness and in her misery, time was immeasurable. It might have been hours, could have been only minutes, before she heard the roar of a returning boat. But this was a throatier sound than the growl of the boy's outboard. A big engine throttled down as it neared the sailboat, then it muttered alongside. *Serendipity* shuddered, then dipped as someone stepped aboard. Clay spoke on deck. "Give me ten minutes, then circle back." The powerboat idled away.

His footsteps sounded on the ladder. "Rikki?"

She didn't speak. When his hand found her, she flinched.

"What are you doing sitting here in the dark, darling? Couldn't you find the matches?"

She heard him open a drawer in the galley, then the rasping sound of a struck match. A light flared. Clay looked at her across the flame for a moment, his eyes narrowed, then he turned to light the lamp. That done, he came to sit beside her. Reaching out, he hooked an arm around her waist and ignoring her resistance, he drew her and her blanket to him. "A problem," he said matter-of-factly. "My deal's coming apart, it looks like. That's the only reason Irene would have tracked me down. I've got to get back to the city and patch it back together."

"My deal's coming apart" . . . It hit her like a sledgehammer—steel smashing down on a frozen lake. Her mind was filled with the crash and tinkle of cascading ice, then she stood knee-deep in a world of glittering, razor-edged rubble. *"My deal's coming apart."* If Clay's takeover strategy was coming apart, it was because of her! Her father had gotten to Oglethorpe . . . She opened her mouth, then shut it again helplessly.

"I've found a guy with a Boston Whaler who'll take me across to Newport. The company jet will meet me there."

She should tell him—*must* tell him.

"I can't take you with me, Rik. The tide's going to be against the wind the whole way. It'll be like fifteen rounds with a heavyweight. The Whaler will make it fine, but it's going to be wet and brutal. You're better off here."

She was better off without him. Better off without the whole dog-eat-dog, power-crazed world. She belonged someplace where things were slow and beautiful, where people made time for each other. Why had she never found such a place? Why couldn't Clay even desire such a place? He sounded energized, excited, ready for battle. He was returning to his real world—this had been simply an interlude, a dream. A willful, foolish attempt to run away from reality.

"I want you to phone the owner tomorrow morning. Explain we had to cut the charter short, and that I'll pay him extra if he'll collect his boat here. You can catch the ferry to New Bedford. Here, I'd better give you some money for that, and then a cab back to Providence." He reached into his back pocket.

"I don't want your money." It all came down to money, didn't it? Or no, maybe it didn't. People like Clay and her father had more money than they would ever spend. No, it came down to power, excitement, a kind of craziness that she would never understand. Never be a part of. She wouldn't live that kind of life. She wouldn't! It would mean nothing but loneliness, partings like this every time something "important" came up—the living, breathing, lacerating knowledge that she was not the important thing in his life.

"Rik . . ." He caught her chin. "Look, darling . . ."

"Get out of my life," she said softly. "You'll just hurt me, and keep on hurting me." *And I'll hurt you! I've hurt you already more than you know.* For without ever intend-

ing to, she had hit him where it would hurt him the most—
in his career. She would have to tell him, should tell him
now, since she wouldn't be seeing him again. Her eyes filled
with tears.

"Rik..." His arm tightened as she tried to move away
from him. "Rikki, forget it. I'm not getting out of your
life." He brushed the hair back from her face, then threaded
his hand through it, holding her still when she tried to shake
her head. "A few more days and this craziness will be over,
Rik. Trust me."

She could trust him to break her heart. In a few days he
would be a winner or a loser, but either way, he'd still be a
player in the game she detested. She would not play that
game with him, would not be a sad and lonely cheerleader
waiting on the sidelines of his life for him, as her mother had
waited for her father. "I want you out of my life."

"Too bad—" He pulled her forward, kissed her unre-
sponsive lips. A low rumbling heralded the return of the
powerboat. Clay stared down at her, not scowling, but as if
he were memorizing her face. "That's too bad, Rik, 'cause
I mean to marry you. I mean to be about as far into your life
as I can get—in every sense of the word. So get used to it."

His determined face was disappearing behind a curtain of
tears. She shook her head blindly. "No."

"Yes." He let her go and stood up. "The boat's coming." Pulling out his wallet, he opened it and tossed several
bills on the table. "I won't have time to see you again until
this is over, Rik. But the minute it's over, look for me... You
can't run far enough or fast enough, so don't even try."

Serendipity rocked as the power boat shouldered up to it.
"Go!" she told him, struggling not to sob. "Go back to the
things that really matter to you!" Curling herself into a
shaking ball, she buried her face against her knees.

For just a second she felt him lean over her, felt the pressure of his lips as he kissed the top of her head. "I'll be
back," he said quietly. Then his feet rapped up the ladder.

Don't leave me! Oh, Clay—don't!

The Whaler revved its engine and rumbled purposefully into the night.

CHAPTER ELEVEN

SHE WOKE late to the cradlelike rocking of the boat. Her face felt tight; she had cried in the night and the tears had dried on her cheeks. She lay motionless, staring at the sunny circles of the portholes above her berth, holding her mind as blank as a mirror upturned to a clear sky. *Don't think. Don't you dare think....* But that was what Clay had told her only yesterday; that was how he'd beguiled her aboard this boat. *Don't think. Just come run away with me.* But you could never really run away from what you were, could you? Clay had not even managed to run away for one night.... Her face seemed to crack, a mirror cracking into a thousand shards of grief, and she burrowed under the blanket again.

Sometime around noon she roused herself enough to get up and get dressed. When she went to make coffee, she found the lobsters in the galley sink, where Clay had left them the night before. They were still alive. After a cup of coffee she found the energy to pry the rubber bands off their claws—gingerly, with a dish cloth thrown over their eyes so they could not see her to pinch—and then she dumped them overboard. "Go and be happy," she told them as they sank into the green depths. Somebody ought to be....

She ought to row ashore, call the owner to come collect his boat, but even entertaining that thought exhausted her. Instead, she crawled back in the vee berth, pulled the blanket over her head and went to sleep—and dreamed of an airport where the man she loved left her again and again and again.

Rikki stayed aboard the boat for three days, not going ashore once, like a child returned to its womb. She might have stayed there forever, but for the geese and her mother.

A flock of the wild geese that lived in the harbor came calling on the third morning and found her in the cockpit. They would not be ignored. They nagged her unmercifully till she let them finish the box of crackers she'd been eating. When that wasn't enough, she fed them her last few slices of stale bread, then watched them sail away, honking their gratitude. There were still some cans of vegetables in the galley cabinets...there was wine and peanut butter, but that was about it. It was time to go. Time to tell the owner where to collect his boat before he set the Coast Guard to searching for her.

And it was past time that she return to her mother. Rikki would have felt guilt, if she could have felt any emotion at all. For today was the day the whole awful struggle must be over. One man that she loved would have lost, and one would have won. Clay had either seized control of her father's company, or her father was buying Clay out at this very moment. Either way, she ought to be in New York with her mother. Her mother might be celebrating, or she might be mourning, but Rikki should be there.

Locking the boat she rowed ashore and left the dinghy in the care of the owner of the fish market. She caught the ferry to New Bedford and then stunned a taxi driver by hiring him to drive her to Providence. It was an outrageous extravagance, but it was Clay's money, and he had money enough to burn. She wouldn't have been so far from home, if he had not taken her there and then abandoned her.

Once she had gotten moving, it was easier to keep on moving. She stopped at her own apartment only long enough for a shower and to call the boat's owner. Luckily he was not there, so she left the message of his boat's whereabouts on his answering machine. Clay could work out any further compensation if and when he ever bothered to pick up his Porsche from the man. Not her problem.

Her problem was to keep moving and to not think. She was on the road by six, her face schooled to a cool, expressionless mask, her eyes fixed on the distance, her mind in a state of suspension that let her deal with car speed and route and absolutely nothing else. By nine-thirty, she had garaged her car in the city and trudged the few blocks to her parents' co-op.

She let herself in with her key. "Hello?" Lights beckoned from the living room. "Anyone home?" The Foo bounded out into the hall to meet her, barking officiously, then leaping waist high in gleeful welcome.

"Rikki?"

"Mom." Rikki stepped into the living room, carrying the squirming poodle.

Her mother sat in her wingback chair, her eyes wide and worried as they studied her face. As Rikki approached she held out her hand and said, "You've heard, then. I'm so sorry, darling."

Rikki dropped the poodle. There was only one reason that her mother would feel sorry for her. "Clay lost?" She had not really believed he *could* lose, somehow.

"Your father bought a controlling share in VenturiCo today, darling. He's down at VenturiCo headquarters now. He's called an emergency board meeting."

Rikki folded slowly onto the carpet beside her mother's chair. Right now her father would be winnowing through Clay's board of directors, replacing those loyal to Clay, deciding which ones he might keep. And then they would vote to depose Clay... "Was it because of... what I told you?" *Oh, please say no! Tell me I didn't do this to Clay!*

Her mother rested a gentle hand on her head. "Clay had agreed to sell Oglethorpe our aeronautics division, to avoid an antitrust suit. So your father offered to sell Oglethorpe the division he wanted for a much lower price, providing he would come in as our white knight. He did, three days ago."

It was the strategy Sam had outlined. Once Oglethorpe tendered for Strategix, that automatically set the date back when Clay could purchase Strategix stock, giving her father his chance to strike first. "And I suppose Oglethorpe will withdraw his tender, now that Clay is no longer a danger?"

Her mother nodded, her eyes shining in spite of her concern for Rikki. Her man had come through.

And this had all happened three days ago. Oglethorpe's entering the fray must have been the emergency that had torn Clay out of her arms. She had done it to herself, if you looked at it that way. Something was fluttering within Rikki's chest, and she couldn't tell if it was a laugh or a sob. She had killed her own love—there was nobody else to blame. And Clay would see it that way, too, once he figured out that she had betrayed him. Or once she told him.

Her mother stroked her hair. "You saved your father, Rikki."

Rikki didn't look up. *Yes, and I ruined Clay!*

"He's a young man, darling. He has time to rebuild."

Yes, he would. She didn't doubt it for a minute. He'd be back on top again. All it would take would be the next eight to ten years of his life to get there—every waking minute of it. He'd be on top again, but at what cost? At the cost of whatever love they might have had. For love took time, and Clay would have none to spare. He'd have more important things to care about than her. But, then, it was her fault, so it was only fair that she lose him, wasn't it?

Her mother stroked her hair again. Rikki closed her eyes, remembering the last time someone had stroked her hair, and the memory brought a pain so sharp she thought it would cut her in two. *Think of something else! Anything else.* "Mom . . ."

"What darling?"

"Did...did Dad ever leave me in an airport someplace, when I was little?" Still staring down at the carpet, she managed a tremulous laugh. "I know it sounds stupid, but I keep having this dream..." And the man who left her was Clay, but he always stood *up*, rising almost out of her view once he'd kissed her.

Her mother's hand stopped. "I imagine he did, darling, that summer he took you to California to stay with my mother. You were four, I think. You don't remember?"

So it wasn't just a dream. Rikki shook her head. "Wh-where were you?"

Her mother sighed, then was silent for a moment. "I was going to take you myself to visit Mama. But I found out I was pregnant just before we left, with the baby I later lost. The doctor didn't want me to fly. Your grandmother had never seen you, and I'd already promised she would, so it seemed like a good idea to let you go on with your father. He had business to do out there. He was going to stay at Mama's for the first few days with you, until you got to know her, before he flew down to L.A."

"But he didn't," Rikki murmured, as the memories flooded in. "Some sort of business came up."

"Yes." Her mother ruffled her hair tenderly.

Her father had left her there at the airport with a total stranger. Those were the hands that held her back, her grandmother's hands. To a child of four, it must have felt—it *had* felt—as if she were being abandoned. Rikki drew a deep, shaking breath. Sam had been right, she *had* been taking all of her hurt from the past and dumping it onto Clay's shoulders. That dream had not been a prediction of what her future would be like if she loved Clay, but a memory from the past.

Or perhaps it had been both. Now she would never know. Not after what she'd done to him.

What she had done... Boneless and awkward she got to
her feet. "Mom, I've got to go out..." There were no
amends she could make, no way to heal the terrible damage
she'd done to him, but still she owed him the truth. Owed
him an apology. Owed him the satisfaction of throwing her
out of his life. She owed him all that.

"Rikki?"

She was halfway to the door already. "I'll be all right,
Mom." Someday. A day too distant from the present to be
even imaginable.

THE CAB brought her to the doors of the VenturiCo building. In contrast to the other buildings along the street its
lobby was brightly lit. As she paid off the cabby, one of the
elevators within opened and disgorged a group of grim-
faced men. They spun out onto the pavement as she approached the revolving doors.

"I need a drink," one of them said bitterly.

"What did you expect?" another interjected. "They
don't call him the Hard Case for nothing."

"But he's competent, and he's fair," said another. "We
could have done worse. Much worse. Won't be that much
different from McCann, once the dust settles." He smiled
at Rikki as she brushed by him and entered the building.

In the midst of a palace coup, security procedures had
apparently been abandoned. The security guard made no
move to consult his list. He gave her a resigned look, then
shrugged when she asked for Clay. "In the auditorium up
on the sixtieth floor, last I heard," he told her and shook his
head. "Never thought they'd take that boy down." He
slouched back to his desk. Through the closing elevator
doors she saw him raise a bottle of beer to his lips. "Damn,
damn shame," he said aloud, and drank.

There was one more head that would roll, if tonight was
not just an aberration born of shock, Rikki reflected as the

elevator rose. Her father would not tolerate anyone who drank on the job.

She heard the noise before the elevator bumped softly to a halt—the rumble of a party in full swing. The elevator door slid open. VenturiCo's elegant silver-gray and black vestibule was packed with men—men standing in circles, pounding one another on the back, gesticulating and talking in near shouts. The hollow *pop* of champagne corks sounded across the room, and someone roared with laughter. Several pairs of eyes swung her way as she stepped into the melee. She was the only woman in sight.

Apparently the emergency board meeting had come to a successful conclusion. This must be how men acted after a battle, with their adrenaline still surging and no target left to hit. All that was left to do was to boast. The flush of triumph, and of liquor, was on almost every face. They all seemed to be talking at once, no one listening, each of them eager to recount his own part in the battle, the telling blow, the shrewd tactic, the feats of endurance, the look of pain on the enemy's face at the moment when he realized he was finished... These were the lawyers, the investment bankers, the tacticians and the public relations men. The board of directors and all the elite of her father's executive staff. And no doubt Oglethorpe—how she hated that name—no doubt he and his people were here to share the victory. They all looked like schoolboys at a post-football-game beer blast.

Her face felt funny, too tightly clenched to smile, out of place amidst all this exuberance. Rikki pressed through the crowd, turning down half a dozen offers of champagne. She slipped into the auditorium that lay beyond the ebony doors at the end of the corridor. Her father's red-brown head of hair topped a huddle of men gathered up on the stage. As she approached, someone slapped her father on the back. He threw back his head and laughed, then accepted a flute of champagne a hand offered him out of the crowd.

She had never seen him like this before in her life. He seemed taller, bigger. His usual authority had kindled to an aura of power, which was reflected in the upturned faces of the men around him. So this was what kept him coming back for more, what had seduced Clay away from her, a taste for this kind of power. A trickle of nausea swirled through her.

"Dad?" He didn't hear her over the congratulations and laughter. *"Dad?"* Still he didn't hear her, but he looked up just then and saw her on the outside of his circle of admirers.

"Rikki!" He plowed through the crowd to reach her and, incredibly, caught her by the shoulders and bussed her cheek. "Come to collect your share of the glory? Let me introduce you to—"

"No!" She stepped back and shook her head violently— that was the last thing she wanted, to be thanked for her part in Clay's downfall. "No, Dad, I just wanted to talk to you."

For once he didn't plead business. "Whatever you say, sweetheart." He plucked another champagne glass off a tray that was being circulated nearby, then drew her to the back of the dais. "What's on your mind? Are you ready to give up teaching and join the firm? I'm sure we can find a place for you. Or can I buy you something? We couldn't have done this without you, you know. You really came through for me!"

She stared at him wonderingly. He wasn't so much drunk as high on his triumph; she had never heard him babble before. "Dad, I didn't—at least I didn't mean—" Oh, what was the use? No good would come of explaining. Then a flash of inspiration cut through her misery. But maybe some good could be made of this mess. "There's one thing you could do..."

"Name it."

"Do you remember what we talked about last week on the terrace—your taking some sort of semiretirement, if you won VenturiCo?"

Some of the merriment left his eyes. He nodded warily.

"Well, you've won. You've made your goal—a company that earns twenty billion in sales. So isn't it about time you paid Mom for all the years of waiting and love she's given you? Could you make some time for her, from now on? I know you didn't promise, but—"

John Casey frowned. "It's going to be awfully busy around here for a while, Rikki, consolidating two companies into one working outfit..."

"All right, I can see that. Mom is going to need six months more to recuperate anyway. But after that? Say starting next spring? Could you cut back to three or four days a week? It would mean so much to her..."

"I know that." He stood very still, not looking at her, not looking at anything. "I don't think I could cut down to three, Rikki..."

"But four? Dad, there's a whole world out there. You'd find something to do if you gave it a chance. Honest you would!"

"You think so?" He delivered it humorously, but there was a real flash of doubt in his eyes.

"I know so. Just give it a chance, will you? Please?"

He took a deep breath, let it out, then lifted his glass to her. "All right. I'll try it. You've certainly been at me long enough." He tipped his glass and knocked the champagne back as if it were a medicinal draught. "Anything else while you're at it?"

Yes, there was, now that she thought of it. "Clay..."

"What about McCann?"

"Is there any way you could... I know he started all this, but is there any way that you might be able to—"

"To help him out? I've already offered him the vice presidency of Strategix-VenturiCo."

"You did?" She could feel her lower lashes brush her cheeks, her eyes were opened so wide. Would she ever understand men at all?

"Why not? I'm going to need twice the talent to run twice the corporation. And they don't come any sharper or more aggressive than McCann."

"But—"

He grinned at the expression on her face. "You can't take these things personally, sweetheart. At least not when you win them, you can't."

"Did he—did he—" But her face fell as her father shook his head with rueful admiration.

"He turned me down flat. Made a neat farewell speech to the board, smiled and tipped his hat, then walked out. Independent cuss..."

Yes, he was that. He might hold no hard feelings against her father, but he'd never consent to be the number-two man where once he'd been the chief. He just wasn't constructed that way, any more than her father was. *Damn them all*... "Do you know where he went?" she asked dully.

"Haven't the faintest. Have you tried his office?"

She shook her head and backed away a step. It was all the opening that several men who had been hovering nearby needed. They pounced on her father, one of them brandishing a notebook and a pen—reporters for some of the financial magazines, apparently. Her father shot her a look of concern over their shoulders. She shrugged, managed something that might have resembled a smile, mouthed "See you at home," and retreated.

The crowd in the corridor was thinning out somewhat, but it had grown twice as raucous. How must Clay have felt, seeing the victors toasting his defeat in his own halls? For a moment she almost hated her father for permitting this celebration. But this was the way of the business world, and perhaps Clay didn't take it as personally as she would have.

But how could he not, when they were dancing on the ruins of his career?

She entered the elevator and hastily punched the Up button before a crowd of men jostled aboard and punched the button for the lobby. When the elevator rose, they all let out a yelp of surprise. "What we doing?" one of them slurred. "Going up to invite McCann to join the party?"

"And get your throat slit for your trouble? No way *this* guy's going to talk to Knife McCann tonight! He might be down, but he sure isn't out." There was a rumble of general agreement, then the elevator door opened.

"Let me out, please." Rikki pushed through the suddenly silent crowd. Someone said something just as the doors closed again, and there was a roar of male laughter.

Damn them all for laughing while Clay hurt! And damn, *damn* herself for making it possible! She spun away and started down the carpeted corridor. Most of the lights had been dimmed on this floor. After the uproar below, her ears hummed in the silence.

He would be gone. If he had any sense at all, he would have walked out, not stayed to see this defiling of his domain. That old sickening feeling twisted in her stomach—he would be gone, and she would be left to search for him hopelessly, desperately. The ebony door at the end of the corridor stood ajar. He'd be gone. But she pushed it open, anyway.

A floor lamp turned Clay's massive desk into an island of light in the center of the darkened room. He was not there. Rikki let out her pent-up breath in a soft sound of desolation. An open cardboard box sat on top of the desk, and another one, sealed, sat beside it. He'd cleaned out his desk already. A lump rose in her throat.

Something stirred in the far corner of the room.

A tall, dark silhouette stood by the windows, staring out over the light-spangled city below. He held his shoulders very straight, but his head was lowered.

Oh, God, she had done this to him! She and no one else. He would hate her forever, but that was almost beside the point right now. The point was that he was hurting. A knife twisted inside her—his pain was hers. "Clay..."

He swung around, but it was too dark to see his face. Had he guessed at her part in his defeat yet? Or would she have to tell him herself?

"So there you are. I thought I'd have to go find you."

He didn't know yet. The knife probed deeper inside her. She shook her head, not sure what she was denying as she walked toward him. "No...I had to come tell you..." The words stuck in her throat like broken glass when she tried to swallow.

"Tell me—?" Clay's hands slid around her waist and locked behind her.

This was the last time he would ever want to hold her. For the last time she gloried in the feel of his hands, their wonderful strength and tenderness. Leaning against them, she had to tilt her chin to see his face. She took a deep breath, then said it all in one rush. "Tell you that this was all my fault...that your deal fell through. It was my fault that Dad heard about Oglethorpe. That's how he got to him." There, it was done. She clenched her teeth, waiting for him to shove her away.

He made no such move. But his face and body seemed to harden and draw inward, as if some gigantic spring were compressing within him. "Yes, I thought you must have."

But if he'd known, then why had he meant to come looking for her? Lips parted, she stared up at him, but his face gave nothing away. She faltered on. "I—I didn't mean to, and I know that an apology won't help, but—" God, if he would only frown, swear at her, do *something*! She shook her head miserably. "I'm so sorry you lost, Clay!"

"Who says I lost?"

Some emotion vibrated in that question, but surely it couldn't have been laughter? She shook her head, trying to clear it. Had something snapped? Was he that distraught that he was simply going to deny the on-going celebration one floor below? "You've lost control of VenturiCo, they're throwing you out of your office . . . you call that winning?"

He propped one hip on the window ledge and drew her closer. "Guess it all depends on what you call winning, doesn't it?"

Something had definitely snapped. So, carefully, humoring him, she asked, "What do you call winning in that case?"

"Well, I didn't get what I started out to win, that's for sure!" His voice was very sane, shimmering with suppressed amusement. The pressure of his hands increased, forcing her gently against him.

Molded to his muscular torso from thigh to stomach, thrilling to the hard stirring of his body against her, she shivered and braced her hands on his chest, then arched back to where she could study his smile. But if he had changed his mind, wanted to win something other than Strategix, could it possibly be— He could only mean— "Me?" she whispered incredulously. Hope rocketed skyward as his body surged against her in silent affirmation. Her hands slid up to grip his shoulders. "You changed your mind and decided you wanted to win me instead, Clay?"

Still smiling, he shook his head no.

Hope exploded like a damp bottle rocket, with a fizzling *pop* and no light at all. Ashes and dying embers drifted down to the dark and muddy earth. No, whatever he'd meant, he'd not meant that. He'd already shown her what mattered to him most, when he abandoned her at Cuttyhunk. Her hands balled into fists as his rejection hit home once again. What was she doing here, letting him hold her with this incredible, wonderful intimacy, when she meant so little to him? The heat in her stomach rose steaming to her face—what an idiot she was! She shoved him to get away, but his arms only tightened around her, locking her in place.

His smile widened to a teasing grin. "No, Rik, I didn't need to win you—I'd won you already. Since that first kiss in the elevator, I've known you were mine for the taking. It wasn't a matter of if, but of when."

"Oh, it wasn't, was it?" The warmth of embarrassment crested and broke over her head in a wave of hot anger. She had come here to offer him an apology and sympathy. She'd known that she would have to face his rage when he learned of her betrayal, but she had never expected him to gloat or jeer like this, not when she was hurting on his behalf as well as her own! Well, she had apologized, and now she would leave. With a violent twist, she wrenched halfway out of his arms, then she gasped as he bent to hook an arm behind her knees and scoop her high off the floor.

"Hey, settle *down*!" Clay laughed, sitting down on the window ledge with her. "You know it's true."

"You—" With her legs kicking over one of his arms, her hands pushing futilely at his chest, she was going nowhere till he let her go. Fighting for control she took a deep and shuddering breath and felt her breast move against his chest as she did so. "You put . . . me . . . *down*!"

But he shook his head. "Not till you admit it's true, Rikki. You're mine and you know it."

Even in defeat, he had not lost a whit of his wonderful self-confidence. Angry as she was at him, she felt the first stirrings of relief and gratitude, and wonder that it could be so. The loss of VenturiCo had not crushed, nor embittered him. He was still her Clay. Better—he was the Clay she remembered. Even so, she was admitting nothing under coercion. "Do I?" she asked dangerously.

"You do." He bent to kiss the corner of her mouth, ran his nose along her cheek, inhaling her scent deeply as he did so. There was something so primal, so claiming in that gesture, that she shivered violently, and his arms hardened in instant response. "You'd marry me tonight, if I asked you." He kissed her full on the lips.

"No." But her head fell back over his arm and she opened her mouth to him with a soft groan of helpless welcome. Her arm slid up around his neck to hug him closer, and she shuddered again. The blood was thundering in her ears, and his heart was hammering against her breast.

"You would!" he crowed against her lips. "You know you would! What a pity they took my Lear jet along with the rest of VenturiCo. We could fly to Las Vegas, be married by sunup..."

"There's always Greyhound Bus..." she pointed out and giggled. He kissed her midlaugh and they finished it together, sharing laughter and the breath to power it and a soaring exhilaration. *He's magic!* she thought, as he kissed her eyebrows, her eyelids, the tip of her nose. Ten minutes ago she would have sworn she'd never laugh again, and yet now...

"So you'd marry me, even though I'm out of a job?" Clay demanded, half out of breath. Though he still smiled, his eyes searched her face, and his body had gone very still.

"Yes," she admitted softly.

"And you'd marry me knowing that I'm at the bottom of the heap, and it might be years of hard slogging before I reach the top again?"

Her own smile wavered. Clay would make it to the top again, she had no doubt, but the years it would take him would be years subtracted from their time together, from their love. And yet— And yet her mother had taken all the scraps of time her husband could spare her, and had counted herself lucky to have them. Maybe no one ever got more than glimpses of real happiness... and maybe that was enough. *For me it will be.* Clay's face blurred before her, but still she whispered "Yes," and then in a firmer voice. "Yes, Clay, I would. I will!"

His chest moved, and she realized he'd been holding his breath. "Then I've won it all!" he announced. "That was the final thing I wanted!" He kissed her hard and long.

"What was?" she gasped, when she could breathe again.

Without answering he eased back on the ledge until his shoulders rested against the frame between two of the plate glass windows. He shifted her weight slightly, cradling her in his lap.

"What was the last thing you wanted?"

"Unconditional surrender." His grin was utterly shameless, but his arms tightened as he felt her stiffen. "Guess you'll have to blame it on the old killer instinct, Rik. I'm afraid I'll always have that."

Yes, no doubt he would, she thought ruefully. It was what made him so vital and so maddening at the same time. She sighed and felt his swift glance at her breasts as she did so. "But I'm still confused."

"About?" He pulled the arm that had held her legs out from under them, then covered her kneecap with the palm of one warm hand.

"You say you won tonight... But you didn't win Strategix, and you think you'd already won me—"

"Think—I *know*!" He chortled and ran his hand down her leg till his fingers closed possessively around her ankle.

"So..." It was hard to think, with him caressing her there. "So...what did you mean, when you said you'd won tonight? Just what did you win?"

"Our happiness," he said simply. Pulling her shoe off, he dropped it, and began to explore the shape of her instep.

"What d'you mean?" she murmured, trying not shiver, bending her knee more so that he could reach her toes.

"That ride back from Cuttyhunk was a bruiser," he told her, his hand wandering restlessly. "The waves were square, Rik, I'd swear it, and it was too wet and noisy to talk. All I could do while we punched through them was hold on for dear life, grit my teeth and think." He caught her big toe and massaged it slowly between his thumb and fingers. "Anyway, somewhere along the way, while the waves were beating my brains out, I guess they knocked some sense back into me.''

"How do you mean?'' She shivered, then smiled at his quick smile of satisfaction.

"Well, I was sure I could make you marry me—and I planned to...'' Clay's hand stopped moving and he simply held her foot. "But the more I thought about it, I wasn't at all sure I could make you happy, Rik, sharing the kind of life I've been leading. And my life was going to get even more intense, once I took over Strategix.''

"But by then, hadn't you lost your chance at Strategix?'' she asked timidly.

He shook his head. "At that point I still could have taken her, but I found myself wondering, 'What the hell am I bothering for?' That day with you on *Serendipity*, I realized I hadn't had as much fun since... well, since we were sailing on the *Princess* that summer. And yet here I was, turning my back on that fun. Going away from the one thing I'd found that I wanted in life—your company. I told myself that I wanted nothing more than to see you happy, and yet I'd left you crying—'' His mouth twisted at the memory. "The more I thought about it, the less sense it made. It didn't make emotional sense, leaving you, and I couldn't even make rational sense out of it—there just wasn't one good reason to do it. It wasn't as if I needed the money, for pete's sake! I've made enough in the past few years to last me a lifetime. I've got enough to buy all the fast cars I'll ever want, all the boats I'll ever sail, enough to feed you and me, and maybe send a couple of kids through college someday... How much more than that does one man need?''

"*No* more!'' She laughed shakily, her eyes diamond bright as they filled, then overflowed. She sat up and hugged him, hard as she could. "Oh, Clay, no more than that!''

"I thought you'd agree.'' Laughing, too, he hugged her back. Heart to heart, they held and rocked each other for a long, long while, then he kissed the top of her head and continued huskily. "So, though I wanted to hear you say that you'd have me on my own terms, it won't be that way—it'll be on *our* terms. I swear I won't neglect you, Rik. I promise."

Too happy and tearful for words, she could only nod. And this time, when they kissed, Rikki did not close her eyes. Beyond his head, she could see the lights of the city—heaven come down to earth and blazing with stars.

IT WAS much, much later, in one of those lulls in the storm of their lovemaking, that she thought to ask. Lying full-length upon the window ledge, she lifted her head from Clay's chest and gazed off at the Brooklyn Bridge, that lovely, dumpy crown of diamonds. "But there's something I wondered about," she murmured, turning to look at him. "You said you still could have won Strategix, when you left me at Cuttyhunk. What did you mean by that?"

Clay reached up to tuck a lock of hair behind her ear, studied the effect, then sighed. "Doesn't sound so nice, Rik...it's a bit of the old killer instinct again..."

"Tell me anyway."

He sighed again, caught another lock of her hair and wound it around his finger. "When you play this game, Rik, you play it for keeps. I don't like surprises, so, for an important situation like this Strategix deal, I always have backup. Oglethorpe was eager to cut a deal with me for part of Strategix—he did it willingly. But what he didn't realize, when he double-crossed me with your father, was that if I'd called in all my markers with his board of directors, I could have had Oglethorpe voted out on the street overnight—or at least threatened to, which would have been just as good. He'd have dropped his lance and backed out of the white knight agreement with your father so fast it would have made your head spin."

"But you didn't call in your markers..."

"No..." Pulling gently on her hair, he drew her down until her lips hovered a scant inch above his. "No, I folded my cards, picked up my winnings and walked away from the table. A wise man knows when to quit..." Reeling her in, he traced the line between her lips with a silken tongue tip. "There's just one thing I feel bad about," he murmured, when she lifted her head for breath.

"What's that?"

"Your father... I know you wanted him to slow down, for your mother's sake, if not his own. Lord knows he took VenturiCo willingly—he grabbed her with both hands—but still I feel as if I've contributed to the problem..."

Crossing her forearms on his chest she propped her chin on them and smiled at him. "It may work out better than you think, Clay." And she told him of her father's promise to slow down.

"Then that's okay." Clay sounded relieved and also ready to dismiss the topic. His hands clamped around her waist. Rolling her gently to one side on the narrow window ledge he sat up. "And now, Miss Casey, shall we fly to Las Vegas and get married tonight?"

"It's almost midnight, Clay! None of the airlines will have a flight, this late."

He swung off the ledge in one lithe movement, then turned and pulled her to a sitting position. "So we charter a jet. I earned over five million this evening, what with my golden parachute, and the VenturiCo stock options I exercised. Not bad, for a loser."

"Not bad at all," she agreed, as he caught her waist and lifted her down. "But about Las Vegas... I don't know, Clay."

His hands tensed suddenly, and he pulled her close against him. "Remember the old killer instinct!" he warned her lightly. "Don't even *think* about not marrying me, Erika Casey."

In spite of his smile, she was very glad that that particular thought had never even crossed her mind. "It's not that at all! But I guess I'm a bit old-fashioned. I don't want a big wedding, but I want friends and family, a pretty dress. Someplace a little more permanent feeling than Las Vegas."

His eyes lost their narrowed look as his hands relaxed slowly. "Sounds good to me. Wherever, whenever you want, as long as it's soon." He reached up to smooth a lock of hair off her brow. "*Very* soon. And in the meantime?"

Standing close as they were, she could feel his breathing stop. Her smile widened—he was not half as sure of himself as he pretended, where she was concerned. "How's the view from your penthouse?" she asked mischievously, then yelped as he caught her waist and whirled her twice around.

"Come see for yourself!"

Laughing, arms clasped tightly around each other's waists, they left his office in darkness and almost ran for the elevator.

EPILOGUE

"WELL, I DON'T KNOW about my wedding present, but the gift wrapping is something else!" Rikki pulled Clay to a halt for the twentieth time that morning, so that she could take in the full glory of a peach-colored hibiscus blossom against a turquoise shutter. Sighing blissfully, she turned to look down the hill toward the harbor of St. George. Bermuda was as wonderful as she'd remembered it, an explosion of color, scent and sound, a feast for the senses. For its present delights as well as its memories, it was the perfect choice for their honeymoon. *We've come full circle,* she told herself and squeezed her husband's hand. "Is it much farther, Clay?"

He smiled without taking his eyes off the boats below. "Just a few hundred yards. So from here on, no peeking, Mrs. McCann." Hooking an arm around her waist, he pulled the brim of her straw hat down over her nose and held it there.

"Hey! I can't see."

"Guess you'll just have to trust me." He tugged her into motion again, holding her close as they walked.

"Hmph!" she sniffed, but it was only mock skepticism. She had learned to take a lot on trust this past week. It was easy to trust, when your mate was so passionately committed to making you happy—and seemed to have an instinctive knack for knowing what made you happy. Recalling the way he'd woken her this morning in their hotel room at the top of the hill, her face warmed and she sighed contentedly.

"All right, under there?" Clay stopped their progress to peer under her hat brim, and to kiss the point of her chin. But from there his lips wandered lazily to the soft skin beneath her jaw, while the hand at her waist grew heavy with desire.

She stood very still—they were in public after all, standing in some sort of square near the water. "No fair, McCann, picking on blind ladies!" But her breath was coming faster in spite of herself.

"What's not fair is looking like that! When am I going to get enough of you?"

"Not for a few years, I hope." *Oh, I hope and I pray!*

"For fifty or sixty," he agreed, a laugh warming his voice. "Okay, we're making a turn here." He swung her gently around on a new course. "Almost there."

She could hear water lapping against stone now, hear the clang and rattle of halyards against masts. They were walking out on the town dock, she guessed quickly.

"Don't peek," he warned her again. Then, with just a hint of nervousness, "I hope you're going to like this."

Rikki hoped desperately that she would, too. Whatever this surprise was, it meant much to Clay. She had seen that in his growing intensity on the flight from New York yesterday, and even more so this morning. There had not been one moment of discord between them since their marriage, and she didn't want to fail him now. But he read her feelings too well for her to ever fake delight. She would just have to pray that he had chosen well, for both their sakes.

"Here we are," Clay told her, and she could read the tension underlying his gaiety. "No, maybe a few feet more." He was half talking to himself. "This is the best angle." He hesitated, and she felt his arm harden. "Okay, have a look." He swept off her hat.

After the shade of her hat brim, the dazzling blues of water and sky were overwhelming. She shut her eyes, then opened them again to find that at the center of her vision, a sleek shape married sea to sky—a tall-masted sailboat moved restlessly against the lines that held her to the quay. Rikki sucked in her breath in a soft sound of delight. Her wedding gift was a thing of grace and sweeping lines—a dream machine in snowy white and lustrous mahogany. She was Clay's dream from twelve years ago in Bermuda. "Oh, Clay!" And then the realization struck home. "It's—oh— it's *Serendipity*!"

Spinning around she threw her arms around him. "Oh, Clay!" She had wondered what he meant to do with his time now that he was retired, had known that he would soon tire of staying in bed most of the day with her. Known that he must have a goal of some sort—he was too vital to live without one. "But how did she get here?"

"Simple. When I bought her, part of the deal was that we take delivery in Bermuda. Her ex-owner sailed her down last week."

So they truly had come full circle. At twenty he'd said he wanted to sail around the world, then maybe sail around again, if once wasn't enough. This dream of a boat would carry them in comfort and safety.

Catching her arms Clay held her where he could study her face. His own was still unsmiling. "But are you sure you're up for it?"

"*Up* for it?" she laughed. How could he think otherwise? She'd be able to find a replacement for her classes even at this date—there was a wealth of teachers needing jobs. To sail with Clay, taking their time, exploring the world, exploring each other... Time enough to love, to play, to adventure...

"Give us five years, Rik," he said hurriedly, "and then we'll come back and settle down, if that's what you want. It won't be too late to start a family five years from now, will it?"

"Sounds about perfect," she said dreamily. They could explore the whole world like a pair of swallows, before settling on a place to nest. They'd have plenty enough money for Clay to reenter the business world, or whatever he wanted to do, when they did return. But first they'd have time to bind fast their own relationship, time to know and depend on each other, time to grow together. *World enough, and time!*

"Come sail with me, Rik."

"Captain..." With a smile, she moved back into his arms and rose on tiptoe. "I'd follow *you...anywhere.*" She kissed the tip of his chin. "Now—want to carry me aboard?"

HARLEQUIN
Romance

Coming Next Month

#3013 THE MARRYING GAME Lindsay Armstrong
Kirra's encounter with Matt Remington on a deserted beach is an episode she
wants to forget. Then she learns Matt is the only one who can save her
father's business—and only she can pay the price!

#3014 LOVING DECEIVER Katherine Arthur
Theresa would have preferred never to see scriptwriter Luke Thorndike again,
let alone travel to New Orleans with him. Yet, although he'd hurt her badly
five years ago, she just couldn't desert him now, when his life was in
danger....

#3015 UNDER A SUMMER SUN Samantha Day
Anne is puzzled by Rob MacNeil's antagonism. After all, he's the interloper,
taking the very piece of land that Anne had hoped to build on. She soon
discovers that Rob is intruding on more than her land....

#3016 A PERFECT BEAST Kay Gregory
Rosemary's enjoyment in teaching is changed when sixteen-year-old Tamsin
acts up. But the sparks that fly between Tamsin and Rosemary are nothing
compared to those touched off by Rosemary's first meeting with Tamsin's
father—the impossible Jonathan Riordan.

#3017 TROUBLEMAKER Madeleine Ker
Ginny was Ryan Savage's sweetheart when he was Grantly's teenage rebel,
before he took off for big-city life. When he comes back five years later,
Ginny, now engaged to an older, more responsible man, wonders what trouble
he'll bring.

#3018 UNWILLING WOMAN Sue Peters
"Just elope," Jess had suggested jokingly to the young woman who didn't
want to marry Max Beaumont—only to soon find herself trapped into
becoming the unwilling Lady Blythe, wife of the arrogant but all-too-
attractive Max....

Available in November wherever paperback books are sold, or
through Harlequin Reader Service:

In the U.S.   In Canada
901 Fuhrmann Blvd.   P.O. Box 603
P.O. Box 1397   Fort Erie, Ontario
Buffalo, N.Y. 14240-1397   L2A 5X3

Have You Ever Wondered If You Could Write A Harlequin Novel?

Here's great news—Harlequin is offering a series of cassette tapes to help you do just that. Written by Harlequin editors, these tapes give practical advice on how to make your characters—and your story— come alive. There's a tape for each contemporary romance series Harlequin publishes.

Mail order only

All sales final

INDULGE A LITTLE SWEEPSTAKES

OFFICIAL RULES

SWEEPSTAKES RULES AND REGULATIONS. NO PURCHASE NECESSARY.

1. NO PURCHASE NECESSARY. To enter complete the official entry form and return with the invoice in the envelope provided. Or you may enter by printing your name, complete address and your daytime phone number on a 3 x 5 piece of paper. Include with your entry the hand printed words "Indulge A Little Sweepstakes." Mail your entry to: Indulge A Little Sweepstakes, P.O. Box 1397, Buffalo, NY 14269-1397. No mechanically reproduced entries accepted. Not responsible for late, lost, misdirected mail, or printing errors.

2. Three winners, one per month (Sept. 30, 1989, October 31, 1989 and November 30, 1989), will be selected in random drawings. All entries received prior to the drawing date will be eligible for that month's prize. This sweepstakes is under the supervision of MARDEN-KANE, INC. an independent judging organization whose decisions are final and binding. Winners will be notified by telephone and may be required to execute an affidavit of eligibility and release which must be returned within 14 days, or an alternate winner will be selected.

3. Prizes: 1st Grand Prize (1) a trip for two to Disneyworld in Orlando, Florida. Trip includes round trip air transportation, hotel accommodations for seven days and six nights, plus up to $700 expense money (ARV $3,500). 2nd Grand Prize (1) a seven-night Chandris Caribbean Cruise for two includes transportation from nearest major airport, accommodations, meals plus up to $1,000 in expense money (ARV $4,300). 3rd Grand Prize (1) a ten-day Hawaiian holiday for two includes round trip air transportation for two, hotel accommodations, sightseeing, plus up to $1,200 in spending money (ARV $7,700). All trips subject to availability and must be taken as outlined on the entry form.

4. Sweepstakes open to residents of the U.S. and Canada 18 years or older except employees and the families of Torstar Corp., its affiliates, subsidiaries and Marden-Kane, Inc. and all other agencies and persons connected with conducting this sweepstakes. All Federal, State and local laws and regulations apply. Void wherever prohibited or restricted by law. Taxes, if any are the sole responsibility of the prize winners. Canadian winners will be required to answer a skill testing question. Winners consent to the use of their name, photograph and/or likeness for publicity purposes without additional compensation.

5. For a list of prize winners, send a stamped, self-addressed envelope to Indulge A Little Sweepstakes Winners, P.O. Box 701, Sayreville, NJ 08871.

© 1989 HARLEQUIN ENTERPRISES LTD.   DL-SWPS

INDULGE A LITTLE SWEEPSTAKES

OFFICIAL RULES

SWEEPSTAKES RULES AND REGULATIONS. NO PURCHASE NECESSARY.

1. NO PURCHASE NECESSARY. To enter complete the official entry form and return with the invoice in the envelope provided. Or you may enter by printing your name, complete address and your daytime phone number on a 3 x 5 piece of paper. Include with your entry the hand printed words "Indulge A Little Sweepstakes." Mail your entry to: Indulge A Little Sweepstakes, P.O. Box 1397, Buffalo, NY 14269-1397. No mechanically reproduced entries accepted. Not responsible for late, lost, misdirected mail, or printing errors.

2. Three winners, one per month (Sept. 30, 1989, October 31, 1989 and November 30, 1989), will be selected in random drawings. All entries received prior to the drawing date will be eligible for that month's prize. This sweepstakes is under the supervision of MARDEN-KANE, INC. an independent judging organization whose decisions are final and binding. Winners will be notified by telephone and may be required to execute an affidavit of eligibility and release which must be returned within 14 days, or an alternate winner will be selected.

3. Prizes: 1st Grand Prize (1) a trip for two to Disneyworld in Orlando, Florida. Trip includes round trip air transportation, hotel accommodations for seven days and six nights, plus up to $700 expense money (ARV $3,500). 2nd Grand Prize (1) a seven-night Chandris Caribbean Cruise for two includes transportation from nearest major airport, accommodations, meals plus up to $1,000 in expense money (ARV $4,300). 3rd Grand Prize (1) a ten-day Hawaiian holiday for two includes round trip air transportation for two, hotel accommodations, sightseeing, plus up to $1,200 in spending money (ARV $7,700). All trips subject to availability and must be taken as outlined on the entry form.

4. Sweepstakes open to residents of the U.S. and Canada 18 years or older except employees and the families of Torstar Corp., its affiliates, subsidiaries and Marden-Kane, Inc. and all other agencies and persons connected with conducting this sweepstakes. All Federal, State and local laws and regulations apply. Void wherever prohibited or restricted by law. Taxes, if any are the sole responsibility of the prize winners. Canadian winners will be required to answer a skill testing question. Winners consent to the use of their name, photograph and/or likeness for publicity purposes without additional compensation.

5. For a list of prize winners, send a stamped, self-addressed envelope to Indulge A Little Sweepstakes Winners, P.O. Box 701, Sayreville, NJ 08871.

© 1989 HARLEQUIN ENTERPRISES LTD.   DL-SWPS

INDULGE A LITTLE—WIN A LOT!

Summer of '89 Subscribers-Only Sweepstakes

OFFICIAL ENTRY FORM

This entry must be received by: Sept. 30, 1989
This month's winner will be notified by: October 7, 1989
Trip must be taken between: Nov. 7, 1989–Nov. 7, 1990

YES, I want to win the Walt Disney World® vacation for two! I understand the prize includes round-trip airfare, first-class hotel, and a daily allowance as revealed on the "Wallet" scratch-off card.

Name_____

Address_____

City_____State/Prov._____Zip/Postal Code_____

Daytime phone number_____
                          Area code

Return entries with invoice in envelope provided. Each book in this shipment has two entry coupons—and the more coupons you enter, the better your chances of winning!

© 1989 HARLEQUIN ENTERPRISES LTD.

DINDL-1

INDULGE A LITTLE—WIN A LOT!

Summer of '89 Subscribers-Only Sweepstakes

OFFICIAL ENTRY FORM

This entry must be received by: Sept. 30, 1989
This month's winner will be notified by: October 7, 1989
Trip must be taken between: Nov. 7, 1989–Nov. 7, 1990

YES, I want to win the Walt Disney World® vacation for two! I understand the prize includes round-trip airfare, first-class hotel, and a daily allowance as revealed on the "Wallet" scratch-off card.

Name_____

Address_____

City_____State/Prov._____Zip/Postal Code_____

Daytime phone number_____
                          Area code

Return entries with invoice in envelope provided. Each book in this shipment has two entry coupons—and the more coupons you enter, the better your chances of winning!

© 1989 HARLEQUIN ENTERPRISES LTD.

DINDL-1